Taboo Sex Stories

Swingers, Lesbian First Time, BDSM, Spanking, Bisexual, Paranormal Threesomes, BBW Erotica, Gangbangs and Much More

Angelo Feldt

rendering of legal, financial, medical or professional advice. The content within this book has been derived from various sources. Please consult a licensed professional before attempting any techniques outlined in this book.

By reading this document, the reader agrees that under no circumstances is the author responsible for any losses, direct or indirect, that are incurred as a result of the use of the information contained within this document, including, but not limited to, errors, omissions, or inaccuracies.

Table of Contents

Table of Contents 3

The Club Citadel 4

The Greatest Deception 21

Waiting for Me 34

A Wife's First Time FFM Threesome 42

The Party 64

The First Time 88

My Friend's Mom 102

You're So Cute 108

The Sexy MILFs First Time Anal Sex 114

Her Halloween Plans 133

The Swingers Club 147

The Special Weekend Extravaganza 168

The Club Citadel

Renee's heart hit her chest so hard that she thought it would explode, right then and there in front of everyone. But nerves are funny things. It was part of the thrill, part of the anxiety about what was to happen. Especially the imminent fate of her long, shiny hay-brown curtain.

The world had no limits, as long as it was safe, healthy and compatible. And hair fetish was a big part of it for some people.

As a long-standing subjection and wife, Renee was very aware of her Master and husband, David's fetish for hair and hairstyles. David was also an enigmatic owner of the Club Citadel, where they played mostly on the weekends.

"Hey, you okay?" Lana asked Renee in the locker room, who almost jumped on her voice.

"I'm... okay, I guess," Renee said, unsure.

Lana smiled to her heartily and let Renee be with those friendly bear hugs without another question. Yeah, Renee needed it the most now.

"Thank you," Renee said. "I'm really nervous as hell."

"Well, it takes courage to agree to this demo," Lana agreed.

It was a ritual at Club Citadel that every third Saturday of the month, a seasoned demo master demonstrates a scene with different things involved. Sometimes it was Shibari, an electric game, any kind of edge game or fetish. Today's demo was: a hair fetish. Master David took it upon himself to demonstrate to the crowd how to do sub climax while giving it the extreme hairstyle that House preferred for Sub.

When David asked Renee to agree to this demo, she couldn't refuse her Master. It wasn't a forceful or blind surrender, but a deep longing to find her own pleasure in serving her Master. This thrill intoxicated her.

"I'm excited and terrified; it's hard to explain," admitted Renee Lana.

"I know that feeling. I felt the same when Xan first picked up the cane," remembered Lana. "But you'd do so well in this demo, Renee. I'm really excited to see it. I'm actually supposed to sit quietly and kneel at Xan's feet all the time," she said with a giggle.

Renee closed her eyes and bit her lower lips. "God! Everyone would be there," she remembered.

It wouldn't be the first time she'd been to the demo, but

it was really important.

"I think you should be in the hallway by now," Lana remembered Renee. "Master David hates being late."

Renee quickly fixed the silk robe around her. "Oh, yes. I can't afford the punishment now. Bye!"

She hurried into the room as fast as her wobbly legs could lift her up and relaxed a little, knowing she wasn't late. But a giant leather chrome-plated barber chair with the right plinth in the middle of the room sucked the breath out of her lungs.

"I can do it," she said to herself, and slowly laid down to the chair.

She knelt down by the chair while people were gathering around. Most of them were homes and submarines, masters and their slaves, and several trainees. Renee was expecting a large crowd because no one had given up watching the championship of a master as experienced as her husband, David.

The low murmur of the crowd suddenly melted when she felt a male hand gently caressing her head. She knew the touch too well and greedily leaned towards it.

David bent a little bit, whispering in her ears, "High course, Sub. Make me proud."

Renee nodded her head. She knew that "High protocol" meant she wouldn't talk unless she did. The safe word was a caveat, but with David, she almost never needed it.

As a neat owner and host, he welcomed the people around him and turned to his beautiful submarine. "Stop", he ordered to give her his hand.

She did it gracefully like a swan. Quickly, the robe was unfastened and removed from her body, leaving her gloriously naked. At the back, he tied her brown hair with a medium length back and helped her climb onto the chair.

Renee twisted a little when the cool skin came into contact with her naked derrière. The chair was extremely large. Quickly, her hands were tied to the armrests, and her thighs were unbuttoned because her legs were also limited.

"Hand tied is optional." Master David turned to the crowd. "But make sure her legs are wide open for your access." To show, he quickly redirected his fingers through her already wet slit several times.

The low noise of consent from the crowd intensified the exhibitor in Renee.

Then, at the snap of a finger, the intern pushed the

instrument cart forward. In the corner of her eyes, Renee took a break on him. She had various pairs of shaving scissors, several hair scissors and at least a handful of appetisers, as well as combs and hair styling products.

He took a wide comb and started brushing her in the most gentle way. "My sub has beautiful hair, as long and beautiful as you all see," he said proudly, and then added, "Although it won't take long once I'm done with it.

His words were like adding fuel to the fire in her nerves. He divided her hair into two ponytails, pinned up with poor rubber bands at the bottom of her head.

With one hand he pulled her hair, and with the other he pulled a new shiny pair of scissors out of the cart. "If you plan to give your subordinate a hell of an experience, I'd advise you to skip the cape." "Let him feel every bit of hair on her delicate breasts. Or cool drops of water when you use the spray."

He brought one of the ponies between the sharp blades of his scissors and started cutting. The movements were slow and purposeful; Renee felt the cold steel at the back of her neck, while the constant "schnick, schnick" kept humming in her ears. When the sound finally stopped, she heard low breath from the crowd.

Women, especially those from other domes, stared at her widely.

David kept his long hair cut like a trophy and then dropped it at her feet. He quietly taped her naked breasts in his big hands and whispered: "You're making a big submarine." Relax. I just started." David was deliciously intimidating. The duality of his actions always kept Renee on the edge of thrill.

He jerked her head off once again when he started cutting off her second ponytail. The ominous sound of scissors through her precious hair danced in waves around her and suddenly stopped again. This time the crowd cheered a little more when the ponytail joined the previous bunch.

"Doesn't she look beautiful without that long hair?" David happily talked to the crowd while running his fingers over her sensitive neck. Renee already had an idea that her 16-inch hair was gone.

Then he took an aerosol bottle and wetted her hair. The water was extremely cool; a few drops were flowing down the neck line and flowing down the valley of her naked womb. "Make sure your submarine's hair is nicely moist. She better feel like you're cutting her beloved hair," David showed.

"Let's give her some fringes now." He combed her face

with a nice piece, and the curtain of hair caressed her chin. A strong grip held her crown, while the scissors began to cut the locks about half an inch above her forehead.

Fragments of damp hair slid down and settled between her chin-lined thighs, tickling. Renee started jumping on the seat to rub her thighs to satisfy the growing damp heat.

David quickly twisted her nipples, telling her. "Did I give you permission to move?"

"No, sir," she said quietly.

Then he picked up the cutters and notified the crowd: "Now the real haircut begins."

Renee swallowed the gas, wondering how far she was going to go. Perhaps if she had reached the climax earlier, all this torment would have ended. But he was ready to pull it off on his whim.

The killer dicks were connected and immediately roared to life. He attacked her back with a vice on the top of her head and pushed her chin into her chest. The cut hair fell all around her and the vibrations on her scalp fell on her toes. An involuntary moaning escaped from her mouth when a sensation started to attack her nerves.

The hair in the back of her head had already been cut to half an inch. Suddenly, she felt her head lean to the side as the menacing scissors were heading towards her left. Behind her shoulders a huge piece of hair accumulated, but some of it slipped back onto her knees again. The slight panic she felt in her bones at the thought of losing a shiny brown mane, mixed with the excitement of the hair cutters on the virgin scalp, was exciting.

"I love how her sweet ears are exposed," David chuckled as he folded her ears and ran the clippers around him. The crowd murmured in excitement as well.

Renee was beating down in a heightened pleasure when suddenly the clippers were off. To add to her mortification, he skillfully ran his fingers through her crack, which was now wet.

"So wet and beautiful," he whispered in her ear and then licked around the rim of her ears to increase the heat.

"Never tell your ward what hairstyle to pick up", he instructed the crowd and started to cut the other side of her head. A strong hug from her Master with a humming machine on her temple drove her mad. Renee couldn't see how short he was cutting her, except that every second she grew a pile of cut hair on her knees.

Among the crowd, Lana sat at her Master's feet. Her Master, Master Xan, leaned slightly and asked her: "How do you want me to do it with your hair, baby? Should I fuck your hair or shave you bald?"

Lana didn't know what to say. Some of them wanted to get the climax while her master banged her head while the other part was scared of shit. What would she look like if she was cut off from the crew?

"Whatever you like, master," she managed to escape.

Xan squeezed himself lightly into her hair and kissed her on the head. "Wonderful, my little one," he complimented her.

In the center of the stage, Master David managed to cut Renee's back and sides off half an inch. At the moment, he was working on her head. He skillfully grabbed a piece of hair between his long, male fingers and cut it off an inch from the scalp. The moistened pieces of hair clung to her cheeks and the whole naked skin, giving her a furious pile of sensations.

"Shall I take my fringe off?" asked the crowd cheerfully. The answer was yes, because everyone liked how she was cut like a sacrificial lamb.

"Yes," David agreed with them. "I don't like fringes either. I'd prefer much shorter hair, like a short, neat look."

Instead of using scissors, he used a clipper over a steel comb technique to quickly cut off the blunt fringes he had previously cut. But he didn't stop there. The comb brushed his hair back, held it between his fingers, and Clippers did the job.

When the top of his head was a little less than an inch, nicely tapering half an inch back and sides, he started piercing short hair with his fingers to move the tiny pieces. Renee finally understood how drastically short her hair was.

"Doms and Masters, if you're not proficient in haircutting or narrowing your gaze, I suggest you have a butcher's cut." All you need is a good hairdresser. But always cut your hair in stages, the fun is all about waiting," he added with a satisfying smile.

"Will you take it shorter?" asked him from the crowd.

"Absolutely, yes," he replied, playing and kneading her breasts. "My beautiful sub had long hair all her life. With this haircut, she won't need a comb or brush for a long time." Electricity poured through her veins on his words when she almost reached the climax.

He stopped the cutters and asked the crowd, "What about number two?"

Renee had no idea what "number two" meant, and neither did the women in the room. But somehow everyone agreed with the cry of joy.

"Very well then."

Another clipper came to life with a growling roar. David stood behind her with a hand hook below the chin to keep his head upright. "My sweet lamb," he whispered. "I'll give you a little clue what I'm going to do. In a moment, you'll get the shortest haircut from your barber."

He unceremoniously drove the cutters over her head - from crown to forehead - like a lot of hair added to the pile. "How could the pile get bigger?" Renee was wondering before the scissors' noise got worse.

David deliberately slowed down his movements, allowing the vibrations on her scalp to give her the chills. Renee was moaning uncontrollably and begging to be released.

To add to this thrill, the Master pushed her down her head in the dominant Western way and drove the clippers over her head to buzz down to 1/4 inch. Renee's excitement had already reached its climax, breathing down the limits.

David, sensing her reactions, leaned in a whisper: "Say goodbye to your fancy combs, conditioners and styling tools, sub".

She reached a climax, then and there. The threads of the tightening nerves melted away, revealing a new wave of pleasure. All the sounds around her were lost, except for her Master's relentless, gnarly tone and terrible haircutters.

And when her brain finally came back to normal, she realized how invigorating the experience was. The crowd noticed how to make subklimax with a simple haircut. It was about control and submission to the master's will. Fear and excitement was a deadly combo, Renee realized.

"I hope my menagerie liked it because I'm not done with it yet," he announced with pleasure. David's excitement was tightening in his pants for what he was going to do next.

"As much as I love keeping scissors on her, I hate being attached to her." With a smile, he took off his guard and clenched his hand on her head again. "Let's take her to another notch," he said.

This time the machine attacked the remaining soft

strand of brown hair on her back, mowing it to zero. "Oh, my God." Renee whispered to herself, realizing he was scalping her.

"No, no, no, no, no," she kept whispering to herself as the next swollen wave of unbridled pleasure began to rise.

The Clippers only approached the occipital bone, leaving white skin behind. Tiny hairs tickled her everywhere, provoking the approaching climax. Then, the balding dicks climbed over her ears to an inch.

"Should I take the side a little higher?" he asked the crowd ridiculously, even though he planned to take it higher and harder. As expected, the crowd agreed.

"I thought so much."

The machine buzzed loudest in her ears when she felt it move up, almost at eye level. Renee tried so hard to imagine what she looked like with her short hair, but she failed. There was no mirror, and she was at the mercy of her demanding Master.

Before David finished scalping her sides and back, Renee was covered in a delicate shine of sweat. Her muscles were tightly rolled, and warm liquid was accumulating between her legs. She discreetly bullied her hips to allow a little friction against her swollen clitoris.

"Let's turn it nicely and clean up now." David chose a different kind of clipper and still mixed the soft beard on the top of his head.

Renee couldn't stand it anymore. A second wave of pleasure went through the roof with vibrating clippers on the scalp that mixed soft beard with bald skin on the perimeter.

"Doesn't it look beautiful when it's clipped like this?" David smiled proudly. His control of the submarine was astonishing.

Renee lost her breath and had a beautiful time. The fear of being cut naked has already turned into a delicious experience she hasn't forgotten before.

"At the last minute," said David. Before Renee could figure it out, she felt the warm foam massaged with hard fingers in the back of her head. Soon it was spread out on her sides, moving upwards. She looked a little weird with the white foam covering her head, except for a small part at the top.

The crowd watched the final stage of the hair fetish demo with great interest. Not only was Renee wet. Lana, whose breasts shaved up and down in shame, was equally wet. The thought of sitting tied up and naked and getting an extremely inductive hairstyle shook her inside. This and her master's hand kneaded and massaged her breasts.

"Don't you dare sleep," Master Xan whispered in Lana's ear even though he knew how dangerously close she was. And then he added another delicious threat: "If you do that, you'll be in that chair, buckled up and naked." And I'd love to shave you bald in front of everyone."

"Oh, God," Lana closed her eyes, wondering how great it would feel. But deep down, was she ready to be bald at the price of an overwhelming orgasm?

Master David, on the other hand, brought a sharp razor, but Renee had no idea. "If you don't know how to use it properly, never use it on a submarine," he warned the crowd with a serious tone, and then he turned to his boat. "I want you to stay put."

He started scraping the foam with small, careful strokes. Any tiny hair was left in the back of his head, the sides were carefully shaved with a blade. The remaining skin was smooth as ever, and there was no hairline around the neck. Instead, only a small strand of hair covered the top and front of the head.

A warm, damp cloth wiped the remaining foam and then shaved afterwards. There was nothing left of her hair that could change a comb or hairbrush. So David took a doll of styling gel and vigorously massaged her head.

The thorough treatment of the rough massage felt like an after-shave treatment.

"Thank you all for your participation," David turned to the crowd. "I'd like to take care of my submarine in private."

He unbuttoned her stripes, freeing her completely. Knowing that her hands were tight, Master David would punch her in the shoulders as she wrapped them around him, and walked out of the room into one of the private rooms.

"May I see my haircut, Master?" She was purring cutely, and he just couldn't refuse her.

"All right," he said and led her to the mirror. "Here's your new look, little submarine."

Renee froze when she looked in the mirror. She couldn't recognize herself. She instinctively ran her fingers through the back of her head and was surprised she was smooth. It was really a very short haircut, as he promised.

As if he was reading in her mind, he said: "It's called Tall and Tight." It's a popular military haircut."

"Oh." That was all she could do. "This is really... really short, Master."

"Do you like it?"

"I'm still working on this whole look," she said honestly. "It will grow back," she said, comforting herself.

"It will grow back, yes." David agreed with the smile. "But I'm not gonna let it grow. I like that tall, tight little submarine on you. Get ready, you'll be scalping again in two weeks."

He kissed her hard, erasing every rational thought from her mind and consuming her body in the most pleasant way she knows.

The Greatest Deception

Molly?" Marcus called her name as he heard her weeping in the bedroom. The door was left ajar and it only took a simple push to open it. He could see Molly laying on the bed, on top of the covers. "Molly, what's wrong?"

She looked up at Marcus and quickly tried to hide the tears in her eyes. "Marcus! I uhm, I'm sorry," she said woefully. "I had an emotional moment."

Marcus walked over and sat down next to Molly with a curious and worried look in his eye. "What's wrong? You can talk to me."

Molly sat up next to Marcus and looked at him for just a moment before looking down. "I can not stop feeling so guilty," she said. "What I did. What I said and how I tried to hide it."

Marcus breathed out and sighed. "What you did with Hunter," he said slowly. "I didn't know how to take it. You were still living with him up until two months ago."

"It was only one time, I really do swear," Molly said sadly.

Marcus didn't want to keep having this conversation. He had only just found out that Molly had cheated on him with her ex during the short seven months of their relationship. She legally lived with Hunter for five of those months due to contractual obligations. Molly really wasn't the type to cheat. She had always seemed reluctant to put herself in any kind of temptation's way. The situation with Hunter was unusual and because of that, her old feelings got the better of her. Marcus found he wasn't even upset about being cheated on. In fact, in an odd way, knowing he had been used in such a way gave him unprecedented thrill. The only thing that bothered him was that Molly wasn't an overly sexual person, which made him wonder if it was something he wasn't doing right in the relationship that drove her back to him.

"I believe you, Molly," Marcus said as he gently rubbed her back.

"I'm crying though because I got that feeling of wanting to cheat again."

Marcus raised a brow to her. "You… have a feeling?"

Molly nodded, ashamed of herself. "I don't know, you know I don't know what it was that came over me. It was just… so gratifying. It was nothing I ever felt before. I am wondering now if there is something wrong with me to think that. I had to be honest with you."

"No, I'm glad you're being honest," Marcus said as he

grabbed her hand. "I always felt like that was something you were missing from our relationship. I didn't know if it was because you were not a very outwardly sexual person or what... but I do think all of this has opened my eyes in some way."

"Really? In what way?"

"Molly, the first thing I thought about when you told me what you did, I got really... really fucking horny."

Molly looked taken aback at Marcus' bluntness. "You... liked being cheated on?"

Marcus shook his head. "I don't know if that is it," he said. "It was just, well, thrilling, so to speak."

Molly looked at Marcus for several long seconds and breathed out heavily. "Marcus, if I saw Hunter again... maybe asked him... would you want to be there and watch?" Marcus looked at Molly like that was the craziest thing he's ever heard, only for his face to quickly change as he thought of the possibility. "I mean, I say that because it sounds like something that could... maybe fix us?"

"I..." Marcus had to pause for a moment as he looked at her. "I wouldn't object."

Molly breathed heavier still as it was clear her heart was pounding in anxiety. "I'll uh, I'll call Hunter..." she said as she slowly trailed off looking for her phone.

"Yeah? Sure," Marcus said as he looked down.

It was less than an hour later that Hunter arrived at the new apartment. Marcus already knew a good bit about him before ever meeting him, as Molly talked about him a lot. Some good, some bad. All Marcus cared about was that this man was going to contribute in a scenario that may just be the sexual experience the young couple needed. They quickly became acquainted as the introductions were brief. Molly had already told Hunter what Marcus knew and how this night was going to go down. Of course, he was far more than eager to be a part of something. He seemed like the kind of guy who would always bring a girl home from the party. The three of them retreated back to the bedroom together as Molly closed the door and dimmed the lights. Marcus took a seat at the chair in front of the vanity and breathed heavily with anticipation. He was already feeling very excited, a feeling that overwhelmed his nervousness. It was clear Molly was feeling the same.

Hunter mostly stayed silent, open to listening to short instructions that Molly would give. She acted almost like she was setting up a wedding event with how meticulous she felt the need to make everything be. Finally, it came down to the moment. Hunter was going to strip Molly down first, and then she would do the same to him. Marcus churned in his seat, filled with anxiety and anticipation. Hunter took his time with Molly's clothes. He casually whistled and smirked as he removed her blouse and her skirt, wanting to get her down to her underwear fast. Molly watched Marcus stare as Hunter began to squeeze her breasts graciously. He squeezed and pinched at her nipples through the bra before lifting his thumbs under the rim and pulling them off like he's probably done many times over. Molly's beautiful breasts popped out and laid against her body as Hunter was quick to caress the nipples as he leaned in and sucked on them hard. Marcus could feel his dick stiffening in his pants from watching.

Molly moaned graciously as Hunter sucked hard, pulling her nipple out with his lips and teeth, really getting into the taste of her skin. His hands rubbed down her sides and over her panties as he dropped down and pulled them with him. Molly gasped as she looked at you, red in the face. It was clear she was ashamed of how much she was turned on by having Marcus watch. Hunter turned and smirked at Marcus with clear joy on his face, uncaring of what their emotions were at the moment. He pushed Molly back on the bed as he pulled her panties off her feet. He spread her legs wide so that he could watch her pussy lips spread. Molly was very wet already, practically dripping. Marcus rubbed his pants watching intensely and taking in the sheer humiliation of it all.

Molly reached down and gently opened her wet pussy hole to Hunter. He licked his lips as he went down on her, his long tongue piercing her cunt and maneuvering its way around her walls. Molly was actively moaning now as her body jolted from the short moments of ecstatic pleasure. She thrusted her thighs back into Hunter's mouth some with more energy than before. Hunter held her down with his hands as he caressed her soft ass and rubbed his thumb over her tight asshole. Marcus raised his brow and sat back in shock at all the things Hunter was so boldly going for that Molly was not objecting to. Molly clinched her cheeks in pleasure as she moaned and visibly moved her body into Hunter's hand and mouth at a consistent rhythm. She looked to Marcus as if to say 'I'm so sorry I love this so much.'

After several moments of finger and tongue fucking, Molly began to shout in ecstasy. Marcus watched as Hunter was able to make her whole body shake with orgasm as he fingered faster and rubbed his tongue wildly over her erect clit. Molly kicked her legs as her thighs rumbled with an eruptive climax. She dropped back on the bed and gasped as Hunter stood up and backed away. Molly leaped up and grabbed his shirt, quickly throwing it off of him. It was no wonder Molly couldn't get Hunter out of her head. He was very fit, and very attractive as a man, even to Marcus. Marcus breathed heavily as he watched Molly rub down Hunter's abs to his pants, quickly dropping them and pulling Hunter's impressive cock out of his boxers.

Molly caressed her tongue up and down Hunter's thick shaft. Marcus could tell she passed the self-shame and completely driven on her sexual desires now. Knowing that made it all the more of a turn on. He wanted to touch himself while watching but somehow felt that it would be wrong to do. He was being cucked. It was supposed to be humiliation and depreciating. He surely felt humiliated knowing how easily Molly was turned into a sexual deviant by Hunter's very presence. He continued to watch as Molly worshipped Hunter's cock. It wasn't even that it was bigger than Marcus's in any way. It was just because it wasn't his cock. Molly tasted every region of Hunter's long shaft, even lifting his cock up to lick and suck on his balls.

Finally, Molly decided to take the whole of Hunter's dick down her throat. She pursed her lips on his head and gradually pushed her head down. Marcus watched in awe and shame as he witnessed Molly fully consume the whole of Hunter's cock into her mouth. She gagged as she deep throated him and shook her head lightly. She pulled out fast for a gasp of air as the trail of spit connected her mouth and Hunter's dick. Immediately she went back in again, fully consuming the whole of the shaft before pulling out halfway and grasping the base with her hand. From there, Molly sucked primarily on the upper half of Hunter's cock, moving her head back and forth to create a good rhythmic friction against his foreskin. Hunter groaned and looked at Marcus with a smirk.

"Do you see how big of a freak she is?" he said with a laugh as he grasped Molly's head and hair and started holding it down as she thrusted back into her mouth. Molly moaned with pleasure as she took in the salty-sweet taste of Hunter's cock like he was a delicious snack. Marcus winced and looked down, feeling like he may just be that inadequate a lover for Molly. "C'mere babe," said Hunter as he grabbed Molly and picked her up, turned her around and threw her down against the bed.

Molly gasped in surprise as Hunter propped her ass up in the air. Marcus watched surprise as Molly hung off the bed standing on her tiptoes to meet Hunter's position requirements. Hunter took his saliva-soaked cock and rubbed it against Molly's dripping wet pussy. Molly moaned as she buried her face into the bed and shook her lower body for Hunter, begging for him to please her. Hunter slid his wet cock up and down Molly's juicy clit. Only after teasing her for several moments did he finally hold his cock still and pushed it deep inside of her open, hungry hole. Molly moaned loudly as her pussy gushed with joy at being filled by such a cock. Hunter grasped her hips as he put one leg up on the bed to properly position and he proceeded to fuck her hard. Molly was just overflowing with juice as she screamed in pleasure into the bed.

Marcus watched, trying to mentally encompass everything. He could see the back of Hunter's balls as is cock penetrated Molly's pulsating pussy. He had full viewing of just how much her body loved everything Hunter was doing. He wanted to please her the same way Hunter could please her. He wanted her to feel this invigorated to fuck him, not just because it was taboo or even forbidden. The fact that he was watching made Molly even more excited, which seemed to have tipped Hunter off that really enjoyed this experiment more than she thought she would. Marcus listened as their bodies slapped together in a rigorous, rhythmic motion. Molly's howling had reached a peak as she did everything she could to muffle her pleasure, remembering that Marcus was watching all of it.

Hunter was prepared to go all out with Molly, not knowing if this was something they'd do again, he wanted to put on a show. He didn't know Marcus very well and didn't really care to. He saw him as weak. He wanted to let Marcus know what Molly was used to and that she prefers strong and dominate men. He pulled open Molly's ass cheeks and exposed her tiny little hole. He spit on it as he continued to thrust and pushed his finger readily inside. Molly was taken aback by the double penetration as her body writhed in pleasure, not knowing what to do with itself. Marcus's eyes widened as he watched, taking mental notes and trying to take it all in.

Hunter pumped Molly several times while fingering her little asshole, matching his cock's rhythm the whole-time in. After several moments, he pulled out to give Molly a chance to breathe. Molly gasped and turned to look at Hunter a bit confused. Hunter smirked and whisked her up fully onto the bed. He crawled up on top of her and spread her legs up wide. He rubbed his fingers over Molly's face as she graciously sucked on them, too into the experience to properly think. Marcus leaned forward curiously as he could barely contain himself watching.

Hunter started to pinch and pull on Molly's nipples to make sure they were as hard as possible. He then situated himself to hold her ass up in the air and spit on her asshole again. He then took his cock and nestled it between her cheeks. Molly looked at Hunter in shock and anticipation as he smirked and slowly pushed his cock deep into her ass. Marcus gasped, never thinking in a million years Molly would be the type to try anal, much less let it happen without extensively talking about it. Hunter was slow at first, really letting his cock push in all the way. He groaned at the feeling of her tight hole closing more firmly on his shaft. Molly's gasps sounded like airless whispers as she squeaked looking at him.

After a few moments of letting the first thrust sink in, Hunter slowly began to pull in and out, letting the full of his shaft feel the tightness of the rim of her asshole. He took two of his fingers and slowly pushed them into Molly's soaking wet pussy. Molly could feel his fingers and cock inside her moving at the same pace in the opposite rhythm. The grinding was so much she climaxed again right there, her pussy seeping with her juices as she shook violently. Hunter gritted his teeth as he started to thrust more and more, getting faster as he did it. Molly's short gasps started turning into longer, more drawn-out screams of pleasure. Sher grabbed and pinched her own nipples and rubbed over her body, unsure what to do with herself. She started viciously rubbing over her clit as Hunter pumped her pussy and ass for several long minutes. Marcus could feel his pants were soaked with his cum as he didn't even need to touch himself to feel the hot liquid force itself out. He was so turned on he could barely contain it, even if that sexual excitement was pushed by his humiliating emasculation of Hunter and Molly's amazing sex.

Molly convulsed again in another massive climatic orgasm. Hunter groaned louder as he thrusted harder. Finally, he pulled out and gasped for air as he started stroking the length of his cock. He pushed the head into Molly's pussy hole as she writhed in her orgasm. His semen quickly filled up her pussy as she made her hot wet mess into a cream pie. Molly looked at Hunter in surprise as she gasped for air. She looked over to Marcus as he bit his lip in over excitement. She looked at him longingly as Hunter pulled away, finishing his orgasm and rolling off of the bed.

Molly grabbed her pussy lips and spread them open to Marcus. "Come and get his seed out of me," she moaned loudly still. "I need you to take in his essence to please me."

Of course, Marcus wanted Molly to be pleased by him. He didn't even take the time to think about what he was doing anymore. He leaped off the chair and rushed over to the bed. He crawled up between Molly's legs as he opened his mouth and took her pussy into it. He waved his tongue around inside her soaking wet hole, cleaning up all of the cum that filled inside of it, both Hunter's and hers. He laid there sucking and drinking up everything as Molly arched her back and came a final time, riding it out slowly into Marcus's mouth as she rubbed her fingers through his hair. After it was done, the two laid back on the bed and looked up at the ceiling, gasping for air. Hunter chuckled and shook his head as he grabbed up his clothes.

"I'm gonna need to borrow your shower before I go," he said.

"Go right ahead," said Molly as she reached down and took Marcus by the hand. "I think we will still be here just a little while longer."

Marcus gasped and nodded, unsure what to fully make of such an experience. He felt the wetness in his pants with a bit of shock as he grasped Molly's hand tightly into his. He looked over to Hunter heading into the bathroom. "Yeah, take your time."

Waiting for Me

I came home from work at noon. Megan (my wife) was already waiting for me and kissed me full on my mouth. Her tongue penetrated me and I immediately knew what time it was. She was horny. She asked if I could help upstairs and so I did. Of course. Arriving at the top, she immediately took my pants off my ass and took my surprised cock passionately in her mouth. She immediately started to blow me good. "Shall we make a quickie?" She asked me, looking horny. "I'm fine, but I'll have to go to work later." She lowered her skirt and slid my prancing cock into her sopping cunt. "What did you do this morning?" I asked with interest. "Fingering and playing with my vibrator. And now I have to get fucked. I can have a whole army." That sounded like music to my ears. She could have an entire army. That was a statement she often made, but it never happened. Fucking, I decided to do something about it. She would get an "entire army." If she really wants that. I have fucked her ready and sprayed my cum deep in her sopping pussy. At 13.00, I went back to work. My cock was glowing and despite my orgasm, I became hornier by the minute. I had to do something with Megan's statement. I wanted to see her be taken by several men once. It has been a fantasy for both of us for a long time. Megan was then laying on her table in her most beautiful lingerie set with her legs tied tight, her sturdy C-cup tits protruded proudly and her raven-black long hair dangled loosely over the edge of the table. This beautiful spectacle finished with her seed-demanding horny brown eyes. "It has to happen once," I muttered out loud by accident. My colleague Brian immediately asked what had to be done. I got a redhead and made something up.

"No, Tyler, that's not what you mean. You want something very special. Otherwise, you wouldn't get that redhead." "Uh, you don't want to know," I said casually. "I tell you my imagination, but then you tell yours. Okay?" "Okay, but you can't make it up to my imagination." Brian said that his wife, Kayla, dreams of doing it with another man. I could not believe my ears. Kayla, a long-haired blond goddess, wanted other men to fill her cunt. Who could imagine that? She was, in fact, almost a haughty woman, who did not dare to approach you. "Come on, now you. Let me be surprised." I told our wish and Brian was not even shocked. He could see it completely. While some 5 Megan were fucking, I would give Kayla the night of her life.

"I hadn't looked at it that way. So, I have to fuck that beautiful girl of yours?" "Sure, that will be the deal. I ensure that Megan has the evening of her life and you ensure that Megan no longer knows what happened to her. Deal?" "Ok. And when will this party take place?" "Tonight. Or is that too fast? Does all of this also have to be recorded on video?" "Is that possible? If so, please. What do I have to take care of?" "You just make sure you have enough beer and put your wife tied up and blindfolded on the table with her most beautiful set on before 9 p.m. I'll take care of the rest. I have my connections."

When I came home that evening, Megan was as horny as butter. She was playing on the couch with the biggest vibrator in her cunt. She had to be fucked. That was certain. "Shall we get a pizza? I don't feel like cooking." She said in a sultry voice. "If I see it that way, you will already cook reasonably well." You are going to have a lot of work tonight." "I usually have no problems with that, you know." After we had eaten and put the dishes in the machine, I asked if she would take a shower. Perhaps a nice start to a wild evening. You already understand that showering was a horny event. We fucked it was a sweet delight and we came together blissfully. After we dried each other off, I took her most beautiful lingerie set from the wardrobe and asked her to put it on. It was a red set with nipple recesses and openwork panties. The black suspender belt and these tights completed the whole. My hooker looked great.

I sent her to the attic to get some "toys" and, in the meantime, smuggled our sm stuff down. While we were making love, we shuffled to the table, it was now 8.45 pm and she laid her legs wide on the table. I put the blindfold on her and told her to stay down. She remained surprised and let what happened. I tied her up so she couldn't go anywhere. There she lay, not knowing what was going to happen. I didn't even know it either. But it would go wild — 21.00 o'clock. The doorbell rang. I went to see who was there. In front of me stood a dazzling Kayla. She was dressed in a summery dress with black, high boots underneath and super hot heels. "Hi, is Brian here yet?" "No, he should be here at any time. We have an appointment." "Yes, I know that. I had to be here too. He told me what to do and went to volleyball practice. They will be ready at 8.30 p.m. and he would come here afterwards. "She walked inside without asking.

When she arrived in the room, she saw Megan lying on the table. She bent over and immediately started licking her clit. "That's nice. A freshly washed pussy always tastes delicious. "Megan did not know what happened to her. She heard a woman's voice and a moment later felt a tongue on her burdock — a great feeling, but strange. She didn't know who it was and had a hard time enjoying it. The bell rang again. When I opened the door, I didn't know what I saw. A whole volleyball team came in. "If those Megan is going to fuck, I am not responsible for the consequences," I told

Brian. "It will be all right. Everyone is pretty careful, but it will be horny. But that's what Megan wants after all." "Tyler, what's happening here?" Megan asked. "You must not be afraid," said Kayla.

"Think a dream will come true. We really won't hurt you. "Kayla stopped by and meanwhile took off her dress. There she stood before me. Her long blonde hair horny and tightly put on. Her blue eyes studied my body and she carefully unbuttoned the buttons on my shirt. With a quick wave, my shirt disappeared into a corner. A few men's clothing was already there at that time. One was already busy eating her. Slowly but surely, the pile of clothing became larger and the bodies naked. Once completely naked, she sucked on my stiff cock.

Slowly but surely, we went to the back room. There Megan was still tied to the table. You could already see that she no longer had a problem with her situation. She was sucking on James's balls while he gently pulled himself over her face. Her big tits were kneaded and sucked by Pieter and John and between her legs; Patrick was pumping his stiff out into Megan's lust cave. She clearly enjoyed it. Around this horny spectacle were still three players pulling their dick. Ready to give the gangbang a great follow-up. Kevin was filming the gangbang with a video camera in a corner. A wrist-thick pasture of over 40 cm dangled between his legs. "When she enters Megan, she tears open," I told Kayla. "You just enjoy it, Megan does that too. She will be able to have it; I can do it. "Suddenly Kayla sucked in my whole dick. I didn't know where I had it. Kayla noticed that I was about to get ready and immediately stopped sucking." You can't cum yet only if I say so. "So that was a problem because I wanted nothing more than to squirt my wacky in that horny face. She lay down on the barstool and told me to stand behind her. Finally, I got into her smooth, shaved pussy. I pumped my by now exploded dick into her fuck cave. At that moment, Kevin came to stand with us and filmed happily. He had clearly done this more. My cock dipped up and down in her warm little cave and again the moment I wanted to spray, Kayla, who clearly enjoyed it, pulled my dick away. "I want to spray Kayla." You will be ready. Only it will be an orgasm like you've never had before. "Megan was moaning and screaming on the table and I saw that a few men had already emptied their balls over her stomach and cunt. In the meantime, the filming was taken over by Brian and Kevin had his jerk licked and sucked.

"I'm just going to help the boys," Kayla said. I stood there. And I was only allowed to watch. She stood between two men and took turns taking their dick in her mouth. "They must be sharp for apotheosis. That's going to be the best thing for the entire evening. "One after the other throbbing dick disappeared in Megan.

She had become an experienced fucking machine in between. Everyone sprayed everything about Megan and after a while, she was covered with sperm. Brian came to stand at Megan and Kevin took her place. He carefully slid the super dick into her. Centimeter by centimeter, his stiffness disappeared between her legs. I did not know what I saw.

Megan lay open and Kevin's whole dick disappeared into her cave. He kept on bumping and Brian happily filmed. When he took his shiny dick out of Megan, his glans swelled and, with firm rays, he sprayed his seed over her open tear. "Come and stand behind me," said Kayla. She was clearly overheated with that entire fuck and started to lick Megan completely clean. "Now, you are going to fuck me and see that you make me cum great." I stood behind Kayla and shoved my dick deep into her. I enjoyed it to the fullest and went into her like it was the first time I had fucked a woman. Megan, who was still blindfolded, was winding under all that pleasure. "Now you're going to fuck me in the ass, my horny stud," she cried wildly. I slid my soaked cock down her ass and was actually surprised how easy it was. She had clearly done this more. I was completely out of the world and was purely busy, giving Kayla the ultimate pleasure. She came screaming.

"Now you give me everything. Spray me completely. "I didn't know what was happening, but I have never sprayed so much all of a sudden. My sperm kept coming and screaming; I pumped her completely full. After all this, Brian put the camera on a tripod and Kayla lay down next to Megan. Everyone stood around the two horniest women I have ever seen. In turn, we sprayed the horny mozzles again and when the last drop of sperm was released and everyone had settled down, the camera was turned off.

We sat in the front of the room and drank a nice beer. "Do you have a PC?" Kevin asked. "Yes, why?" "Then, I leave the camera here and you can view everything again." "Can I now be released?" Megan asked, exhausted. "No, when we're gone," said Kayla. "You are going to have a horny night. Take a look at the video we made. You will enjoy it. Take it from me. "After a few beers, everyone went home. I released Megan. "It was like a dream come true." She hung up exhausted and looked great horny. "Do you want to know what you did?" "Yes, please." We went upstairs and I connected the camera to the PC. What we saw was huge. The film only showed the faces of Megan and me. The rest were left out of the picture. Megan really did not know who they were and I decided to keep it that way. I don't have to explain what happened while showering. But we enjoyed each other for over an hour and the warm water.

A Wife's First Time FFM Threesome

Carrie wasn't ashamed to let her husband Jimmy know that her biggest fantasy was being with another woman. But Carrie had never seriously contemplated doing it in reality. What she doesn't realize is that Jimmy has taken a lot of notice and now he's come home with the perfect fantasy woman. Carrie is nervous but Sonja takes over and soon the reality is better than any of Carrie's fantasies have ever been.

I stared at Jimmy. "What?"

He looked at the floor and pushed his floppy fringe back off his face. "Carrie, you always fantasize about it, I thought you might want to make it come true?"

I'd been with Jimmy for ten years, we had three kids heading into their teens, and now he wondered if I wanted to have sex with a woman? Did I? Could I? "I'm not sure what to say. Are you serious?" I'd had a couple of wines, and the kids were away for the weekend, so Jimmy and I always got half tanked and had the noisy, sweaty, inventive sex we didn't get to have with kids in the house.

He shrugged and looked like he wished he'd not

mentioned it. "Forget I said it. I don't want to ruin our weekend. It's a fantasy, I get it. No pressure."

I sipped my red wine. I had always used that fantasy as a way to get to orgasm quick, imagining another woman's tongue and fingers were touching me and not Jimmy's. He even played along with by talking dirty about it.

But then, we talked a lot of smack when drunk and horny, and we agreed whatever was said wasn't to be taken literally, it was fantasy and very much heat of the moment. After ten years of relationship, it was fun to explore things with the person I trusted more than anyone in the world, and he'd never broken my confidence or made me feel silly about what turned me on at any given time.

A lesbian experience was on my go-to list most of the time, so I could understand him asking me, I just never expected it to actually come up as a serious topic. He did have my attention, though. "Is that what you want?"

His face colored up and he looked even more sheepish. "If you do…I mean, I dunno…it always turns you on so much, and that gets me hot and thinking about it."

I drank the rest of my wine and refilled my glass. "Are you bored with our sex life?"

"No, no way. It's amazing."

"Would you want to touch this other woman?"

"Absolutely not. It'd be an all-girl show. I'd just watch, if you wanted me to."

Now the thought was in my mind I found it hard to shake. Could I? I actually wasn't sure. I had a lot of attractive friends, but no way was I attracted to them in a sexual way. Besides, I'd have to see them again, and I think that would be awkward for me. If I did this, it had to be with someone I wouldn't meet on the corner or out shopping.

So, that meant under the right circumstances, I would act out my fantasy. Is that what it meant? I wasn't sure, but the thought wasn't turning me off, it was turning me on. But it couldn't just be any woman. I had certain criteria my fantasy followed, and I'd never seen a woman around here who looked like that. I'd come across a few in magazines and some in real life kind of came close, but that was a fleeting thought only at the time. I saved my female exploits for my sexual fantasies when I was alone or with Jimmy.

"What's made you ask now?"

"We've had some VIP clients come through this week. One of the women seemed like she'd be your type."

"My type? God. I don't have a type, I'm not into women like that, it's a fantasy."

"Alright then, your fantasy type. Whatever you call it. I'm telling you, she's perfect."

"Even if she is, it doesn't mean she wants us creeping on her for a sexual fantasy. She probably has a husband and kids at home. She might have a string of lovers for all we know."

Jimmy shook his head. "She's single, and by all accounts, she enjoys male and female company."

I stared at him. He'd pried into her personal life already? Maybe he's the one with the fantasy problems. "You're unbelievable." I still had to smile that he'd been so thorough.

"You know we always do deep research on potential clients, we like to offer them something to suit all of their needs while they're in town."

"For the business, yes, but not for fulfilling your wife's sexual fantasies."

He grabbed me and held me close. "I can't think of a better reason."

Jimmy knew me so well, he kissed me the exact way I liked, and I let him. He was taking care of me as always. The kiss left me breathless, and I was already needy just thinking about my idea of my fantasy woman coming to life.

"She's tall, athletic. Her name is Sonja. Long legs, darker skin, short hair. She's perfect for you."

My breathing had gotten deeper, and my pussy now throbbed for attention.

"Her ass cheeks are high and tight. A pair of perfect, round globes. I know how you like that, you've shown me in pictures before. I think hers are perfect for you. Her breasts are large. I couldn't see if her nipples are what you want, but I bet they'd be close. Long and suckable. Plump areola."

I was really starting to squirm now. "Stop it. You're just teasing me."

"I swear to God this woman is just what you want." He slid his hands down the front of my pants and massaged my mound. I opened my legs so he could slip a finger between my lips to touch my clit. It felt so good, I groaned, and my fantasy was alive.

"This is her touching your clit. She's naked, and her body is strong but soft. She knows a woman's body. Knows what works as only a woman can." Jimmy rubbed my clit, and I began to buck my hips for more.

"She's dark, exotic and her tongue is pink and long waiting to lick you out hard and drink all your sweet, sweet come."

My body shook as I let the fantasy wash over me and Jimmy took me closer and closer to orgasm with his hand. "You suck her breasts, pulling hard on her nipples, she does the same to you. Her body pressed against yours. Her scent all around you. You want to come so bad right now."

"Yes, yes I want to come. Make me."

"Will you meet her for me? Will you think about letting her touch you and taste you?"

"Yes, Jimmy. I will."

"Tonight?" His hand moved back and forth, and he sank his fingers inside me, and the heel of his hand pressed against my clit. "Say yes and I'll set it up. Tonight you can have your fantasy come true."

I kept grinding onto his hand, needing more. I was so close to orgasm I'd have said yes to anything to get release.

Jimmy increased his movements. "Say yes, Baby. Her hot mouth and long tongue can be doing what I'm doing with my hand right now. Then you can lick her pussy, she'll be sweet. You'll make her come hard."

"Yes!" I crumpled against him as the orgasm hit me with the thought of making her come. "Yes…yes. Oh fuck, yes. I want to make her come hard."

Jimmy played with me until the last of the orgasm had passed. I was so keyed up, and I'd came hard and fast.

"I'm going to set this up. Here, tonight. Wear something really sexy and she drinks red wine, so choose our best bottles. She's only in town a week, so you ever have to see her again after that. This will work."

"Will you stay if she's into me?"

"That's up to her. If she wants me around, I will but if she doesn't that's fair. I'm happy to step out and see you get your fantasy."

"You're an incredible man, Jimmy. I'm so nervous."

"No pressure, just us having drinks. I'm sure we'll soon know if she's into it or not." He leaned in a kissed me, and then headed for the bathroom t wash up and head back to work for the afternoon. "Let's keep dinner light and fresh."

"Sure. I'll make finger food."

Jimmy raise his eyebrows, and I laughed, he never missed an innuendo. "I'll see you soon. If you have time, go buy something new. White, almost see-through, that you can be naked under. I think if she gets a glimpse of your sexy body, she won't be able to resist."

I smiled. "I'll do my best."

"I'll be back at seven." Then he was gone, and I wasn't sure where to start. I checked the fridge. I'd need a few things to make up some quick canapes. So shopping for food and the perfect outfit first. Then back here to do the food and bathe. I'd just had an orgasm, but was aching with need again. I'd be so ready when they got here. I hope she said yes.

****

I was nervous and excited. I almost felt sick. Was everything good enough? Was I good enough? I'd pulled my golden blonde hair up and made a messy bun on top of my head. My neck was really sensitive, and nothing turned me on more than having it exposed and ready to be touched and kissed.

I never added earrings because my earlobes being sucked and bitten was another huge turn on. I added a freshwater pearl choker to bring attention to that area. The dress I'd found was perfect. It was chiffon and had many layers. You could see the outline of my naked body underneath, yet it wasn't completely exposed.

The floaty skirt swirled around my ankles, and I added some strappy, high heels. The neckline plunged between my large, rounded breasts and exposed the top of my flat, tight stomach. I worked out daily to keep in shape. I did add some lace panties because I was worried my arousal would be sliding down between my thighs otherwise. My heart was hammering as I arranged the food platter and opened the wine to breathe.

What would she be like? I couldn't wait to see her and see if Jimmy was right. Then I heard his voice. "Carrie, we're here. Come and meet Sonja."

I took a deep breath and wondered what on earth this would all lead to but I also knew not thinking into the future was the best way to handle this. I rounded the corner to the entranceway, and every part of my body was zinging as soon as I saw Sonja. Holy fuck, she was perfect.

Jimmy had that 'I told you so' look and for the first time I welcomed a woman I never knew into my home hoping to fuck her in every way I could. It was almost embarrassing the way that I wanted her from that first flash of her dark eyes, and those long legs went on forever.

Her eyes had an exotic shape, almost feline. I caught

a drift of her mango and coconut scent, and I wanted to put my mouth on every part of her body. "Welcome, Sonja. So excited you could be with us…I mean come…come for dinner…" Argh. Why did everything sound sexual? This was worse than any teenage awkwardness I could ever remember. I took another deep breath and Jimmy gave me an encouraging smile as he walked past me.

Sonja walked towards me and placed her hand on my bare arm. "I'm delighted to be here." She gave a slight rub and followed Jimmy into our open lounge and dining area.

I was sure my knees would give out from her touch which still tingled on my arm. Sonja was interested, and my pussy was aching for her already. I knew this was going to happen, and I needed a red wine to relax me a little more. I didn't want to ruin my fantasy coming true because I was so nervous. I had to act like I was cool not a nervous Nellie.

"What do you drink, Sonja? I'm having red wine, but we have whites, spirits, or even beer." My voice wasn't reflecting how I shook inside, thank God.

"Red is fine."

"That's great because we have a twenty-year Shiraz, and it's wearing some big boots," Jimmy grinned and poured a glass from the breakfast counter.

"Perfect," Sonja said, and her smile made my day.

"Take a seat, table or lounge, make yourself at home." I went and grabbed her wine and gave it to her as she sat on the sofa. Her skin glowed against the pale eggshell blue leather. She patted the cushion beside her as she took the wine from me and her finger touched mine briefly, and I felt the heat race to my face. Shit.

Jimmy walked over with our two glasses and handed one to me as I sat awkwardly beside Sonja. I gratefully took it and had a gulp. The warmth of the strong wine went straight to my veins, and I felt braver right away. Jimmy sat in the armchair practically opposite us, and he sat back and looked very comfortable. This was really going to happen. I could feel the sexual vibes rocketing from her. I was so glad I'd worn panties because I'd never been more ready for anything and I'd have soiled my pretty dress.

"I love your dress." Sonja sipped her wine and smiled.

"I found it today. Yours is awesome. Red really suits your darker skin."

"Thanks. What do you do?"

"Pardon?"

"Work? Do you have a profession?" Sonja's lips were so plump and thick I could hardly concentrate on what she said.

"I'm an artist. Oil paints."

"I wish I had creativity like that. I'm a lawyer. But I'm on a week's vacay, to relax. High pressure job and I can't…enjoy myself in my own city. Too many prying eyes wanting the scoop on the ice queen."

"That must be painful."

"Not really because I get to come meet people like you, and Jimmy." She reached out and traced a fingertip down my cheek and the side of my neck and shoulder. "I get to do whatever I want with anyone I want."

I sucked in a breath. She was so hot and smelled so good, and she wanted me. "That sounds nice."

"I'm not one for beating around the bush. Have you been with a woman before, Carrie?"

I shook my head. "It's a fantasy of mine. Jimmy thought you'd suit it very well, so he suggested I make it a reality."

"Clever, Jimmy. One of my fantasies is taking a woman for her first time."

My heart was in my throat, and the sexy look in her

eyes thrilled me to the core. I drank some more wine and placed my hand on her knee. "Do you mind if Jimmy watches?"

"I think he deserves that much for bringing us together." Sonja finished her large glass of wine and nodded to Jimmy for another and I did the same and gave him my empty glass.

Sonja scooted closer and cupped my face in her hands. "You're beautiful." Her mouth was moving ever closer, and I held my breath. When she touched her lips to mine my desire exploded inside me, and I know I began to shake. This was happening, and she was my perfect fantasy woman.

Her tongue pressed to mine, and I caressed mine against it. It was so amazing having the soft lips of another woman kissing me. Our bodies closer now, I entwined my fingers in her shorter hair and opened my mouth further. Sonja deepened the kiss and made it more demanding. The dancing of her tongue over mine had me groaning into her mouth.

She touched me at the crevice of my breasts, sliding a hand under one breast and rubbing her thumb across my nipple. I almost came right then, and I pulled her even deeper into the breathless kiss and arched my back for more of her touch. I couldn't believe this was happening so fast.

Sonja was a woman who knew what she wanted, and even better, she knew what I wanted. She pulled out of the kiss I was still so desperate for and left me gasping for air. "You're needy. I can't believe no woman has ever given you what you need."

"I…I never…I mean…it was only dirty talk we used. For fun."

"Lucky for me. Now, that's a pretty dress, but if I'm going to fuck you properly, I'll need you naked. Now strip."

I stood up feeling sexy as fuck and pulled the dress off over my head. There was nothing else except the scanty underwear.

"Jimmy come hold her legs wide. I'm gonna blow her mind."

I stared at Sonja. I never expected that.

"Lie down on the sofa. Lift your legs up and Jimmy can hold you open for me. I need your cunt spread good and wide, so I can get at every bit and fuck you deep with whatever I choose."

Was soon in position and I knew my pussy juice was running down between my ass cheeks. Sonja dipped her fingers inside me and slathered my juices all over my clit. "You're so wet, such a dirty, wet bitch." Sonja slapped my ass cheeks over and over, and all I could do was bite down on my lip and groan. Her other hand played with my aching clit and the harder she slapped me the faster she used her fingers on my sensitive bud.

I arched for more and met Jimmy's gaze. He was behind my head and holding my legs back. "Is that good, Babe? Do you like her doing that?"

"Fuck yes, so good. So, so good."

"I like watching you. Your cunt is so swollen and ready for her. You're beautiful, Carrie. So fucking beautiful." He leaned over and gave me a careful upside-down kiss.

I cried out into his mouth when Sonja sank three long fingers deep inside me and slapped my clit again and again. I was at her mercy, and I loved it. Jimmy finished the tender kiss and pulled my legs back harder, so my ass was off the sofa and Sonja had full access to my most personal parts.

"I'll make you come hard. So hard you'll think you've turned inside fucking out. You'll squirt your sweet juices all over me." Sonja moved so she could fuck me deeper and harder with her finger and she pressed the inside upper wall of my cunt, and I felt a pressure build like never before.

She lowered her head until she finally clamped her generous mouth over my sex and suctioned to me. The tip of her tongue flicked at my clit hard and fast and each time I cried out she fucked me harder and deeper. Her mouth was doing insane things to me when my orgasm let go, I screamed as I came over and over so hard.

My body and mind were at her mercy, and no sooner was the orgasm over, and she was licking me dry with her thick, long tongue.

"Holy fuck, Sonja. Amazing. So good." My body was still shaking inside and out, and all I wanted to do was taste her. "Let me try. Let me taste your pussy. Get naked for me."

Sonja nodded to Jimmy who slowly lowered my legs. "That was the sexiest thing I've ever seen. I'm so fucking hard right now."

Sonja stood and stripped the clothes off her body. She was everything my fantasy had desired and more than I could ever have imagined. Large ripe, pendulum breasts with long nipples perched on bulbous areola, ready for the taking. I latched onto one and sucked as hard as I could.

Sonja groaned, and I was pleased she enjoyed my amateur attempts to please such and experienced lover. I worked my hand over her pussy and between her wet pussy lips to touch another woman's vagina for the first time. It was like hot silk. I slid my fingers inside her tightness, and her rippled inner walls clung to me.

I had a need to stretch them and so I plunged three fingers inside as far as I could, and she bucked onto my fingers begging for them to go deeper. I could have fucked her like that forever, but I wanted to taste her.

"Let me taste your sweet cunt."

"I have to watch this." Jimmy moved around behind me as Sonja laid back on the sofa and opened her candy-pink pussy to me.

I just stared at her glistening pussy for a minute and breathed in the sweet scent of her. I parted her pussy lips with my hands and drove my tongue deep inside her. Jimmy swore behind me, and I got on my knees and cocked my ass at him hoping he'd get the message. I needed to be fucked as well.

Jimmy grabbed my hips and slid into me, and I used my tongue inside her a little longer and then slid it up over her swollen, hot clit. I'd never imagined a woman could taste and feel so good. I moved my tongue over her clit and around, sucking now and again while I drove my fingers deep inside her in short bursts.

Sonja said my name, encouraging me to keep going to try everything. "Yes, Carrie, yes. Just like that. Fuck me harder, use all your fingers, I can take it, baby."

I did as she instructed and I felt her cunt tighten around my fingers. I held them inside her worked on licking her clit with the flat of my tongue rasping over her delicate nerve bud.

"Yes, yes. Like that. Harder, harder. Oh, Carrie, you're making me come. Making me come so hard. Lick it, mother fucking lick that clit."

I did, and as I went harder, Jimmy held me fast by the hips and fucked me harder than I'd ever felt before. "Yeah, Carrie, Yes baby. Make her come. God, so sexy. I'm gonna come inside you."

I was carried away with the moment as one came in my mouth and the other in my cunt. Sonja came so hard she almost squeezed my fingers out of her. It was divine to make another woman come. Better than any fantasy. I moved upwards kissing her soft belly and caressing her clit softly with my fingers now.

Her tits were so delightful, I had to taste them and feel them in my mouth again. I grazed my teeth over her nipple, and she groaned as she came down from her orgasm high. I moved my hand and held my sodden fingers up towards Jimmy. Both Sonja and I watched him as he sucked and licked my fingers dry and moaned his delight.

"That's for being a good boy. Your treat." I felt so powerful right now. Watching Jimmy obey me was amazing but I could follow that up later. "Now, go sit down like a good boy. Sonja and I have some unfinished business." If this as only going to happen once, you better believe I was making the most of it. He sat in the armchair, and I turned and pulled Sonja close to me once more.

"You're so sexy. Better than any fantasy. Thank you for making mine come true." I kissed her sensual mouth, and our tongues glided hungrily over each other's. I fisted my hand in her hair and pulled her head back to make my kiss harder and more demanding.

She responded by kissing me back hard and then pulling away roughly and bending me over with my hands planted on the sofa. "I'm not done with you yet. That pretty pussy will come hard again for me." She sank her fingers into me from behind, and it sent shockwaves through me.

I can't believe I could still want it so much. But I did. I parted my legs to brace myself as she landed a stinging slap to my ass cheek. Her fingers filled me hard as she fucked me with them. I was still wet from Jimmy coming inside me, and each slap took me higher. She stopped slapping and started to play with my clit.

"Spread your legs wider, slut. You know you love it. You're my bitch tonight."

I began the inevitable climb towards orgasm again. Sonja knew just how to work my aching clit. Soft then firm, around in circles, easing off and then firmer again. My body began to tremble, and I wanted her to never stop. "God, yes That's it. Just like that. Fuck me deeper."

Sonja pressed her fingers down on the wall of my cunt and massaged firmly on that magical spot. I felt like I was going to explode into a million pieces. I'd never had such an amazing finger work inside me before. Someone who knew just where to find the sweet spot of a woman. I loved it, and though I wanted to come again, I never wanted this to end either. As if she knew that, Sonja stopped working my clit, and just finger fucked me, working on my g-spot. Now and again she'd give a circle of pleasure to my clitty. Just enough to get me begging for her to make me come again.

"Please, Sonja. Let me come."

"No. Not until I say."

"I can't take anymore."

"Yes you can and you will. You'll come when I make you, and not before."

"I need to come right now. Fuck. Just do it. I need it." The pressure still built impossibly. I was so close to coming, but I couldn't quite make it. I rocked and writhed my hips back and forth trying to get the contact I needed to set me off. Sonja laughed huskily. It sounded so sexy. "Please. Sonja. Please just let me come…I can't take anymore. I need you."

"Beg all you want. I'm not ready for you to come yet." Her finger touched lightly onto my throbbing clit, and I was so wet, I'm sure she almost had her whole hand shoved in my cunt now. I loved it. I groaned and swore and screamed for her to let me come. She just laughed and when I'd almost given up hope of her making me come she pressed onto my clit and rubbed me just where I needed it most.

I lost it. I was convulsing and coming so hard I had tears rolling down my face, and all I could do was cry out. My body was shattering from the inside out. But then as much as I couldn't come before, now I couldn't stop coming.

Her fingers inside me and carefully working over my clit made the next orgasm roll in almost immediately. I gripped the sofa so I wouldn't collapse and Sonja began to work me hard again, and my third orgasm came like a lightning bolt through me. I just cried it was so good, so intense, and so different to anything I'd ever had before.

I couldn't hold myself up anymore and next thing I was lying in her arms as she kissed my wet forehead and I glanced over to see Jimmy smiling, and he'd clearly come again.

Sonja gave me a long, sensuous kiss and looked me in the eyes afterwards. "Carrie, you never have to fantasize again. Whenever you want me, just let me know."

The Party

Douglas and I have been a loose couple for a year or so before we graduated from high school. About a year later, we got married, and nobody was surprised about this. The brother of Doug, Russell, was our best man. He's one year younger than Doug. Russell was in the army, and we even had a wedding a month earlier because he was out on a two-year trip. We had a great wedding party that night instead of going off on our honeymoon. In fact, the party was for Russell.

He had some beers and a few drinks like all of us, and all the girls were dancing with him, so I got myself in a few. He was kind of close, but Doug didn't say anything about it. I was wearing a long wedding dress that was thick and heavy so I wasn't worried about it. He was still living with his mom and dad at home. They left earlier than we did, Doug, and I took him over after the party. We stayed a little until he settled down. The next day, he shipped out. It was almost two years ago.

Doug and I had a great honeymoon at the resort, and over the last two years, we bought a house and settled down. He had a fantastic job that paid more than decent, and I had an office job three days a week. We spoke to Russell every time he had a chance to call, and then one day he said he was coming home.

Everyone was excited and eager to get him back safe and sound. He was going to be in the States for a couple of years.

When he got home, we had a welcome home party. Most of the men had beer and the women had wine. There were a few skirt cousins and a few mothers, and we all seemed to be dressed as a guy. I was wearing one of my short shift dresses. We've had to dance with him a few times. I don't think there were so many women available where he was working. It was clear when we danced that he was well aroused.

Doug said it was probably going to happen, and if I could ignore it and let him have a good time, it would be okay with him. Often, as we danced, Russell seemed to bounce between my thighs. Some of it fascinated me. All seemed to ignore the fact that he was getting so excited. I didn't really mind that. It was the Doug's, and now it was mine, too.

We took him out for dinner a couple of times over the next week. Russell was more experienced, he was more focused. He was not repressed, or worried, or anything like that. He was average, but he grew up. I think the army is doing that to you. He smiled and laughed and told us stories, and it was good to have him with us. I liked Russell, but I was always mindful that he was Doug 's brother, and I tried to relate to him without it becoming a problem.

Russell had been gone for 60 days because he couldn't take any of the places he was, but he said he was just going to take 30 of them home and the rest of them traveling and looking around. He had a lot of money, almost two years worth since there was no place to spend it. About two weeks later, on a Friday, I got home at 3 o'clock and at 3:30 o'clock Russell drove up the drive. After opening the door, and he came in and gave me a kiss on the cheek.

"Hi Diane," he said to him. "Is Doug home yet? If you guys don't have any plans I figured I 'd drop over for a while."

"At loose ends?" I asked. "Russell, there should be some available with all the girls you went to school with. This town can't be that empty, even after two years."

"Ok, there are a few left over here and there, but mostly," he said. "I guess my standards got a little higher. A few or so won't give me the time or day. High school stuff, I guess. So, how's Doug 's life?"

"It's absolutely the best thing," I said. "He's a really nice guy and he's doing well to take care of us. I 'd be lost without him. He 'd have to be here in around an hour if you could stick around."

"There's no surprise," he said. "He's always taken care of me. He's always been there when I needed him. I never fully realised that until I got shipped out. I grew up in a hurry. I just had to stay alive. Sorry , I didn't plan to go there. I told myself I wouldn't. Sure, I will stick around. Thank you."

I worked in the kitchen, and Russell was sitting in a swivel counter chair. I got a beer for him. He swiveled around watching me as I turned about, and we were talking about high school and teachers. I was still wearing my work clothes, a summer shift that was a little short, but I could bend over alright, and I wasn't worried about showing him too much, just thighs. It was a summer shift that kept me nice and cool. All the shorts I could wear with the company made me sweat and feel uncomfortable. I had the others I only wore around Doug. Often I didn't wear pants with transitions, but I didn't have a problem with anyone seeing anything, so I didn't look like I didn't wear pants.

Doug came home a little after 4. He changed, and both of them headed towards the den. It was pretty cool in the house. Russell was wearing long polyester sweatpants and a matching jacket. In between, he had abs peeking. Doug had the same thing, except his legs were just above his knees. They both had plenty of room for comfort. They were nearly the same weight and height, muscular and pleasant to be around.

We had salads and tiny rib-eye steaks and a couple of potatoes on the island. It was really good to both of them. I've always felt very close to Doug 's family. When we were done, Doug gave Russell a beer and shuffled it off to the den to relax while we were in the kitchen.

Doug said, "He seems to be a little sad. I don't want to use the word lonely, but something like that. Would you like to dance with him, or would that be too obvious? He seems to like dancing."

"If you want to, I don't mind," I said. "Every time he's danced with me so far, he 's excited. If you don't mind that, he 's sure."

"Any man on this planet would have done the same thing," he said. "You 're a beautiful exotic woman, and he's probably going to be able to detect that like I did."

"Are you not trying to show me that you are?" I said.

"Perhaps a little bit," he said. "Perhaps it will get him to think more about all the girls he knows. It might help."

When Doug and I put our den together, we made it more comfortable and comfortable. The curtains kept out the heat, and the lights gave it a subtle and private look. We wanted it that way, so we could have a little fun in it. We picked out the sofa with great care , making sure nothing seemed obvious. I was talking about it when we joined Russell in the den. I 'd have to be sure it wasn't that obvious. Doug brought a bottle of wine, and I brought the glasses with him. I loved wine, but I was going to be pretty sure I didn't get tipsy.

Doug didn't give me any specific guidelines, so I decided to let him monitor Russell like he did so far, so it's not going to be a problem. The thing I was worried about was that after two years of marriage, I was really comfortable with sex, and maybe I let it go too far. Ok, I guess Doug knew that. I was just trying to do my part. That's more or less why I accommodated Russell fitting himself between my thighs when we were dancing. I wasn't worried about it just because it was all right with Doug, and it was his brother. Doug would still avoid anything that was a problem.

My shift was a button in the front, but the buttons weren't that far apart. I'm probably supposed to put on my shoes, but I didn't think that Russell could say, and he couldn't see anything anyway, so I didn't. I picked out all my short shift dresses, so the material dropped tightly between my thighs, should I were to spread my legs for the smallest amount, and there was enough material to cover me, and then some. I've had a solid bra and thank heavens for that.

Russell had already finished his beer, so Doug poured

some wine on us. Russell enjoyed the wine. Me too, man. The glasses were the big ones with a wide stem base, so they wouldn't be so easy to turn around. They only looked hollow with a finger or two or three of the wine. Doug started some kind of soft music.

"We usually listen to some relaxing music after a day of work," he said. "If you want something more lively, let me know. Sometimes Diane and I like to dance in the evenings. I shouldn't say it's going to get us ready for bed, but it's going to get us ready for bed."

He might have said something other than bed, but I think it was to get the war off Russell 's mind. It might take a while.

"Relaxing music is all right," Russell said. "That's a nice set of speakers. Very nice sound. Isn't that the Wharfedales?"

"Yes, I used them," he said. "Actually new, great quality."

Doug got up and took my hand and took me to the side of the sofa, where we had more room, and we started dancing a really slow, sensuous dance. After a while, I melted in the way I usually do, and Doug was already a little hard. Not completely, but more than normal. His hands were in their usual place at the top of my buns, so he could feel the tip of my ass crack. Well, I liked it.

He liked it, man. Russell was a little quiet but smiling and watching and sipping his wine. I had the distinct feeling that he was a little embarrassed.

Doug whispered, "The first dance is the odd one. After that, it's more natural. If he's a little nervous, he 's going to calm down."

"You seem to be concerned about him," I said. "It'll be all right. He's with his family, and besides, he's excited about me when we dance, so I'm not totally opposed as long as you're comfortable with it. He said you've been taking care of him for a long time. That's probably what you're doing now."

After a bit, we broke up and sat down and sipped some wine. Russell was still a little quiet, so I got up and took his hand, and we walked past the end of the sofa. I figured I 'd end up dancing twice as much, but most of the time I sat at my job and I was slim as the guys were, except for their muscles, and I rarely wore myself down. When we turned back to see, Doug was on his way to the kitchen or the bathroom. Russell was still excited, so he jumped a little between my thighs, not totally up but making an impact.

I was thinking that I might be able to lead him into an unexpected orgasm. He would have passed it, and that would have been it. We could still have a nice night of dancing in the area. I got a little more around his neck and slowly let us get closer to each other. Not excessively, but I could feel more of him, and I figured he might feel more of me. His hands were right where Doug was, at the top of my ass crack. He might have been following Doug's lead.

"Doug is doing that," I said. "I just love his hands on the top of my buns. Sometimes he rubs down and pulls me tighter. Russell, I'm not going to break if you want to be a little closer. Rubbing body parts is a good way to enjoy each other."

"I would, but I don't want to be too obvious," he said.

"I wouldn't mind, and I don't think Doug 's mind," I said. "I think he's trying to teach me something."

With my arms around Russell 's neck, my shift was pulled up a little and split under the last button. Without any pants on and holding the flap open, I could feel him right against me with only his exercise pants in between. I didn't think he was wearing any underwear either. He probably didn't know I didn't know, but he might have felt some heat. I 'm sure I could.

Russell kissed my cheek gently and, after a few moves, his hands crossed my buns, just above my ass. I was taking a little break at that. My shift was a little thin, and he pressed right up my ridges, moving around with each step. I gave him a kiss on the cheek, and I put my head on his shoulder. I wish I didn't have a bra on now. When we turned around one more time, Doug was back and gave me an 'ok' with his thumb and finger. He had to see where Russell's hands were, and how close we were, and what was rubbing against my forehead, and he still gave an 'ok.'

I'm 5ft8.5 and the guys are 5ft11 so we were almost at the same height. I wasn't a little kid downstairs, my forehead was pretty big. I pulled my arms out of his neck and walked around his waist, and he got around my neck. I let my hands slide down under his top on pure heavenly skin. Slowly up under his top and back and forth, and a finger in the back of his trousers and across his thighs. A couple of times when my back was pumping into Doug. Very gently, but he did it. When his back was in the direction of Doug, I pumped back about as much.

We turned around, and I let Doug see me under Russell's top in the back, and a finger or two dips in the top of his pants. Doug just smiled, so I think that Russell and I were doing what Doug wanted or expected. The music was of great speed and volume. A few slow turns, and Doug had his legs on his foot stool relaxing, so I knew he was good to let us go like we were. Russell was soaking me up, and I think I was also doing a little soaking. It was clear that Doug loved me to provide some of what Russell wanted. It had to be fun for him, too. He 'd like to thank me later in bed tonight.

When Russell and I turned around, it was a very slow turn, because we were dancing very slowly, and sometimes my back was going to Doug for a minute or so. The next time my back was towards Doug, I slipped my hand down the back of Russell 's pants and fingered the top of his butt crack. Not too far down, but I happened to push a finger down a little. I didn't think I was too far down his butt crack for that, and I was surprised. I thought it was a little too far away, but Russell didn't react, and Doug didn't know.

A few turns later, Russell took a finger down my butt crack, pushing some of my shift. It wasn't going to pull out, and I was not able to just reach back and pull it out. I was trying to open my butt so it would drop out, but it wouldn't. We started to turn around again and I figured Doug was just going to get up and dance with me when he saw it. We danced with my back to Doug for a few minutes, and Doug had to see it, but when we turned around again, he smiled at me.

We stopped dancing, and I was sitting down. Russell

was going to the bathroom. He was really tough on the looks of his pants, but he was sticking up rather than over or down. At least he wasn't poking his pants out. Doug and I were talking about more or less everything but me and Russell. In the end, Russell came back and I went to the bathroom. I caught the smell of sex as soon as I opened the door. Russell was having an orgasm. I was very pleased that it had worked. I was also glad to have been able to do that to a man other than Doug. The washcloth was hot, so I knew that he was a gentleman. I used a different washcloth and cleaned it up.

Doug and Russell and I sat around and sipped the wine and laughed and had a good time. A nice change from the silent sexual teasing we did. I totally had a nice sexual high with Russell and Doug because he was watching me with another guy, brother or not. Most of the time, I found that Doug was watching us closely. After 15 or 20 minutes passed, Doug got me up for a dance. Doug and Russell were very similar to what they did to me. When things were calm, I tended to let them enjoy me while I was enjoying them. I could also feel Doug under my front dress flap. He didn't appear to be wearing any underwear either. I thought maybe he'd get me more excited about Russell. I got wet when I was excited, but not excessively, so there was no problem. Well, I could go on.

"You were perfect, I think," he said. "You've always had great instincts. Are you okay with him? I don't want you to be uncomfortable. I'm not tired at all, we could do this for a while if you're enjoying yourself."

"I 'm fine," I said. "As long as you want. He's doing the same thing you 're doing to me. I've stuck my fingers in the back of his pants so he might want to get under the back of my shift. You could slip your fingers under the next time we turn around to see what it's going to be like for him.

"Okay," he said.

We took our time and slowly turned around, a little further away from the sofa. When my back was away from Russell Doug, it slid down my buns and curled up under my change. I think he thought I had a string at first, then he slipped a little between my thighs and crashed into my ridges and knew I didn't have any pants on. I just felt him pause for a moment, and then he slipped his hand back on my shift.

He said that. "I love that feeling. Diane, I think he can do that if it's not a problem for you. I think the sexual high is great for all of us. We don't often get that chance with family. We 're probably more concerned about each other, but it never hurts to ask."

"I love the feeling as well," I said. "When I feel it, it doesn't matter whether it's you or Russell. It's highly sexual and almost takes my breath away. If you don't mind his fingers there, it's fine with me. If we dance with his back to you longer than normal, his fingers are usually where you are. I don't know exactly what he's going to do."

"Okay," he said. "Attempt not to have an orgasm yet."

Doug and I sat down for about 10 minutes while I was drinking some wine, not a lot. I got Russell 's hand, and we started to dance. It's been more than half an hour, so he's probably going to get competitive again. I was going to wait until he pushed back under the front of my shift before I had him under the bottom. He was hard in a couple of minutes, and he rubbed nicely. I was wrapped around his neck with my head against his back, but now and then we exchanged light kisses, open lips and touching tongues a few times, particularly the last dance. My breasts were wrapped with a solid bra so I could put then into his chest so he could feel them, not squashed instead.

Sometimes his hands were on my hips and he twisted my middle one way while he twisted the other slightly. He often plopped back and forth over my clit with a dick that was so hard. Slowly, I moved us out of the sofa about four or five more feet, and I turned our backs to Doug. We weren't jumping all over the place, opting to shift our feet slightly in one position and we slowly turned around so it looked like dancing rather than making it stand still.

I took my arms out of his neck and moved around him just above his knees. He was around my arm. After a few moments, I slipped a hand in his pants and cracked his ass, curling fingers beneath, so I could feel his cock. I used a single finger and scratched it here and there. He moved himself further towards the front of my shirt.

I kept doing that for a little bit, so he knew it was on purpose. I pulled my hand up and we exchanged our arms and hands again and slowly turned around. It didn't take a long time before his fingers came under the bottom of my shift and straight up between my thighs to my ridges and down to the entrance of my vagina.

He knew that I loved it because I moaned right in his ear, trying to work a little on his finger. The nerve ends of my vagina were on fire. I could see Doug over Russell 's shoulder, and he was very excited. He knew that his brother was feeling me up. Not too many, but he's been there. Oh, at least Russell had an orgasm, so he was good to go. We slowly turned around again and again, and he did it two more times. When that happened, I spread my legs a little more. I'm pretty sure Doug will see my legs come out. We kept my back from Doug, and Russell wasn't worried about working with me.

Doug wasn't just sitting there, and he wasn't part of everything. He danced with me as much as he did to Russell. The next time he got up to dance, we didn't get off the end of the sofa as we did before. He slipped his arms around me, and we were dancing right there. After five minutes or so, he got up again under the back of my dress, and Russell could see Doug's hand coming up underneath. After a while, Doug came back to the bottom of my buns.

Doug said, "Would you mind if I pulled your dress up so that Russell could see your buns? I think he 'd get a kick out of it. I think he's really tough again. I'll keep it up for a while so he can fix it in his mind. He'll definitely be thrilled. Maybe we could dance around a little while he's looking. He'll love your buns shifting around."

Well, that didn't surprise me so much. I mean, we've already broken that kind of barrier, and that's clearly what Doug wants to do for him.

"You know him a lot better than I do," I stated. "Whatever you think he 'd want is all right. I'm glad to help. He's done what you've just done, just so you know. I could feel his finger right at the entrance to my vagina."

Doug slowly danced me back and forth from the front of the sofa and turned us around so that my back was to Russell. My legs were about three feet in front of Russell. Both Doug's hands slid down my buns, and I felt that my shift was pulling up , going up my waist. Some of them pulled up the front, but Russell couldn't see it. We danced in place for a few minutes, then turned around like normal and just kept going, with the back of my shift going up at my waist. When my back was to Russell, I spread my legs a little, but not so far that it seemed too excessive. Doug shifted his legs a few times, so I could.

The next time we turned around, Russell had a hand to play with his dick on top of his pants. We caught each other's eyes, and both of us smiled. The whole thing was awesome. I was hoping that Russell could see how wet I was from the back. I could see a dark spot on the front of his pants from his foretaste. Slowly he rubbed and jacked his cock in his pants. We've been up like that for around five minutes, maybe longer, I've been really ramped up and I haven't kept track of that much.

Doug said, "I think you're really turned on. Have you

had fun?"

"I'm really turned on, that's for sure. Russell is, too. Did you see him playing with his dick? He's not going to have an orgasm, he's got one when he went to the bathroom, I could tell. I guess he couldn't stand it."

"He deserves it after almost two years gone," he said. "What do you think about letting him see your face, too? Is that too much?"

"I'm so hot," I said. "Does he mind that? I don't mind that."

"I think he's going to like how wet you are," he said. "I'm going to move us together then turn you around and slowly unbutton your dress. Is that okay? Just sway back and forth. If you feel like opening your legs to him, go ahead. He likes to play with himself when he's hard to enjoy when he's looking at you."

I kissed Doug on his lips and nodded 'yes' a few times.

I couldn't talk about it. My level of excitement was way up there. I haven't been running down my leg yet, but it could happen. We kept dancing a little while as Doug moved us back to Russell. My bare butt was really getting next to him. He could only reach out to finger me. We stopped, and instead of Doug turning both of us around, he turned me around. Russell was wearing his pants just below his crotch and his dick out and up. He was exactly the same as Doug, hung. Slowly, he jacked himself, his bare dick.

I squeezed myself as hard as I could, and I felt that Doug was starting to unbutton my shift from top to bottom. He came down to my belly button, and I got nervous. Russell was the first and only other man to see me exposed. Russell was laughing slightly while he was playing with his cock. I swapped to look into his eyes and look at his dick sticking up. He was circumcised as Doug was, and his head was smooth and shiny. His ball bag was a little solid and sticking out of his crotch. It's been a fantastic sight.

I felt Doug's fingers down, and I started to open my legs a little at a time. My legs ran into Russell's, and he pulled them back and slid them between mine and moved down the sofa, so that his dick was out close to the edge and up like an erotic statue. By then, Doug was pushing the sides of my shift out of my shoulders. He kissed me on the neck and the cheek, unhooked my bra, took it off, and put his arms around my waist. I've put my hands on his. By then, my legs were open enough for Russell to have an excellent view. Doug took his hands from beneath me and placed them on top of me.

He said, "I think he's going to really like this."

Slowly, he moved my hands down either side of my pussy and pulled it out so that Russell had a complete view. I've been tilting my front out for him. Well, I just couldn't help it. His hands were trapped between mine and his cock was a foot or two away from me. He pushed his dick through his fingers a few times.

"This is absolutely erotic," Doug said. "Why don't you slide your knees and straddle him? You can tease him all you want. He'll let you go. It's all right. He's not going to do anything you don't want to do."

I wasn't completely in a trance, but I was nodding 'yes' while I was sliding my knees on either side of Russell's hips. I felt him almost instantly up my ridges, and my ridges slipped down on either side of his dick as I pushed him in. The amount of electricity was very high. When he jacked his dick, I felt his fingers on me. Our eyes have been closed. When Doug and I went to fuck, and he was almost in me, I had to kiss him. I haven't realised it for a long time, and one day Doug told me that. I kept doing that out of necessity.

I leaned over with Russell's dick and fingers playing on my pussy and clit to kiss him out of habit. Doug slid both of his hands down under me on each side of my pussy, pulled me open and lifted me slightly, and I followed him. Russell moved his dick back and forth, and I felt my head go down my clit and into my ridges. Afterwards Doug pulled out his hands, and Russell's dick literally sank almost to the end of my vagina. I started to lift and drop. I couldn't get my hips to work right, they wouldn't rotate. I leaned forward, and my tits came to his chest, and he took off his top. I felt that his pants were pulled out against my bottom. Doug took off his pants and took off my socks.

Russell and I were completely naked on our couch. I saw Doug placed a pillow on the end of the sofa for a moment, but it didn't really register. We began to fuck a little bit more. I glanced over the back of the sofa in a little bit and saw Doug again in the kitchen, but he didn't really register. I got my arms around Russell 's neck, and he was on my buns. The fuck was absolutely thrilling and one of the most sensual and erotic moments I've ever felt.

After about five minutes, Russell tilted me over to the sofa so that my head was able see the pillow. He had to pull out for a while, but he was fast back in between my thighs. We both got adjusted and aligned against each other and got back on track. He hasn't been seeing my nipples and breasts for a while. We've just been too busy processing this fuck, and it's been a while before I could lose my mind to think. Doug had already done this for Russell. No telling how many girls he's got for him. I didn't mind, this whole night, this was mind-boggling sex. I knew I wasn't going to quit until he had two years worth of quality fucking. I figured I 'd always be open to Russell, too. That was all right, too.

He went a long , long time before Russell had an earlier

orgasm. We had to get it out of our minds so we could play with passion. Doug has never disturbed us. I had four orgasms, three of them almost explosive. Doug had another one, right at the end, when we were almost worn out. A lot of semen. We fucked for an hour and a half without stopping for something, the last half hour just for fun. After having a shower and all three of us went to bed and had a threesome all night long. I got to suck Russell's dick and I got some sperm. I didn't say anything to Doug, but I think he knew it.

It's never been a problem between Doug and I, so I think he was a little shocked that I went along with him. Not shocking, but more grateful and appreciative. It's obvious that he loves me as much as his brother.

One more time, about six months later, I got to fuck Russell. Doug wasn't home that day, but he knew it. That night, he thanked me.

The First Time

When Lily said it, she watched Cameron's face contour into a frown firstly of confusion then of some other emotion which she could not easily place. It was a plan that had been two years in the making, since the first time he had spoken to her in sophomore year and now barely two weeks to graduation and with the help of Susan, she had finally had the guts to say the words to him.

His lips opened and shut, struggling with an out-pour of words that never really made it out of his lips. Lily quickly looked at Susan for support. Susan was more sharp-eyed, one who seemed to impress her conviction on another without the unnecessary fuss of fear. With Susan, Lily thought it was either of two options. It was either Cameron would agree to her request, a really simple one, of course, he was already in her apartment drinking alcohol and playing games with the girls since the early hours of the evening. Lily swallowed hard. Cameron's eyes never left her body. Hers did, distractedly, finding comfort in the little details scattered about in the nightshade of her apartment.

The bottle of alcohol, which was placed between the trio, was her most frequent fascination. Drunk halfway and the little shot glass by it like a lieutenant, Lily wondered if it has been necessary a move to convince Cameron she liked him. Susan had said it would help. She had naively assumed it was to help with Cameron but slowly and more certainly, the stains of tipsiness on her own being led her to an understanding of who it had been for. She had been a different person that evening and she loved it even though the confidence was nowhere near where she wanted it to be.

Cameron turned from her for the first time since the revelation and looked to Susan for any signs of collusion between the girls. His handsome profile made Lily whisper a subdued purr.

His fine brown hair, stained with strips of more colorful gold always neatly cut even like his nails. His eyes were a dreamy black, one which allured and drew in attention when he demanded it. His nose was the perfect shape, not so aquiline and not so large. Lily knew she would kiss those lips of his for a long time if he let her. It had been two years and she had just asked.

He was a magazine model who had fallen out of the front cover by error, Lily thought to herself the many times she lay in her bed going through his features in her mind, refereeing the wrestling between temptation and confidence. Confidence had won this evening with some help from Susan's presence, but whether it had won Cameron over was yet to be seen.

"Do you mean what you just said?" Cameron asked, his right now jumped with the query.

Lily hesitated, looking to Susan and then back at Cameron in a quick motion of her head's swing.

"Yup. She does," Susan answered, sighing and made the obscene gesture with her hands. "She just dared you to have sex with us. Now, your call!"

Lily could not tell if it was the confusion that made the boy all the more handsome, but she thought his face was paler as he waded his way through the thick pool of indecision towards the shore of a conclusion. It was a long haul but he pursed his lips. She knew his fingers had come upon the first sand of that shore.

"You ladies are beautiful but do you think I'm the one...?" His words dried up in his mouth and his shoulders dropped. Lily sensed he was having to doubt himself and she wondered if her hunch was true.

"Look, Cameron. If you don't want to I'd understand," Lily muttered in easy resignation.

"No. No," Cameron said, sharply. "I want to. I think it would be awesome. It has to be better than beating my meat to sleep like I do every other evening."

Lily's alarm met its match in Susan's face, but Susan's was more subtle. Cameron shared the concern when he sensed he had spilled more information than was necessary.

"You don't have a girlfriend, Cameron?" Lily asked, quivering but with more confidence than she had a few minutes ago.

"I don't think anyone would want to go out with me. They think I'm a nerd," Cameron said, giggling.

"You're smart and that's OK." Lily swept her butt across the floor and towards him when Susan winked at her. "I've always thought. Never mind." She canceled the thought.

"Are you a virgin?" Susan asked, complementing the end of Lily's speech.

"No. But I don't get sex often," Cameron revealed without hesitation, and in truth.

"So you know what you have to do," Susan hinted, and snatched the bottle of alcohol from the floor and took a swig. "Hmm," she called with a grunt, passing the bottle to Lily who also drank and passed it to Cameron.

Cameron's hands trembled when he started to drink and Lily calmed him by putting her hands on him. She then took the nearly finished alcohol bottle and placing it back on the floor.

"Here, let me help you with that shirt," Lily said, moving astride his legs and sat on it.

She leaned towards him to kiss his warm lips, and the world in Cameron's eyes faded to a cozy black.

They kissed intimately for minutes for an eternity, both basking in the pure delectation that their innocence with each other provided when Susan joined them when breaking up the lovemaking. She cupped Cameron's head in her palm and culled him away from Lily and in her direction. Cameron thought Susan's kiss was less warm than Lily's had been; being more direct towards the point of lustfulness which his boyish desires craved. With Lily, it was lovemaking. With Susan, it was fucking.

Cameron's heart raced as he caressed Lily's butt as she sat on his hands, both legs about his sides and kissed Susan. He half expected the show to be over before they even got a chance to get it on, scarcely able to bring himself to the realization that it was him with both the girls engaging their passions. The sense of surrealism of the events hovered over proceedings even when Susan let his lips go. He returned to kissing Lily and pinching her ass closer and spreading them apart in a rhythmic stir.

He tapped her ass once and Lily giggled in his face. He opened his eyes just as she did hers as telepathy had communicated on both their senses. Her wide eyes from his position held something deeper than attraction and for a moment he thought it was just the alcohol clouding his sense of judgment, but the more he thought about it, the more it made sense. If she was not at least attracted to him, she would not have proposed such a dare.

He recalled some of the moments vaguely when she might have hinted towards his lure and he smiled as he pieced them. Lily placed her hands on his chest and withdrew from him, biting her lower lips seductively as she did.

"It's a beautiful thing to find love isn't it?" Susan teased and they both laughed. "I'm uninterested in that. Now, enough of that funny shit and let's find me some release."

Lily pushed her hands down Cameron's body, picked the hem of his shirt and slipped it upwards by his shoulder, then above his head.

His bare chest was beautiful, even though she had had no expectations of his body, she was pleasantly surprised. His chest had been well exercised, the muscles on it already divided into two finely separate pieces. She ran her hands over it and her body shook from delight. Susan was out of her clothes and bra, wearing only her pants. Lily stood up to help herself out of her clothes and Susan replaced her on Cameron's laps.

Susan did not kiss him. Cameron had not expected to be kissed. It was something about her, a certain roughness that he was in to entertain. It was the thrill of unattached sex, she owned the vibration of the kind of girls that would fuck you tonight and not even say hello to you when you met them in class the next day. People like Susan were incredibly attractive for the sake of their coldness, male or female versions of them and with her on Cameron's laps feeding her breasts into his lips, he understood why.

Cameron placed one hand on Susan's back for support and the other on her chest to better direct her breasts into his mouth. His hand on her bare ass was a sensation he struggled with. He kissed her pink smallish nipples and sucked on them blindly even as Susan moaned, massaging then with both her hands until the mound was firm. It wasn't long before the nipples were erect and Lily returned to them.

Susan pushed Cameron slightly and he fell on his back. Susan directed the exercise from her point above him, her body made into an obstacle that cast itself over the bleak light so that a halo was about her frame like a divine being. Her firm breasts and erect nipples called and Cameron moved to answer when she stopped him with her body across his chest.

"Blow him," Susan said to Lily who quickly get to the task without delay, slipping his trousers off his waist as Susan fed him her nipples one last time. It was time for something else.

Lily gasped when she pulled Cameron's pants to his ankles and returned to sampling his cock. It was easily one of the biggest she has ever seen, curvy and lengthy, the type that was sure to find sensations in a woman's body wherever it might be. Susan turned to her at the noise and when she too turned to see it, she laughed. Susan leaned back and stroked on it together with Lily, and when Lily put her lips on the penis, Susan left it to her.

For Cameron, it was as though the several heavens of pleasure known to man had descended on Earth and it's manifestations to him was in Lily and Susan. Lily's mouth on his cock was the most pleasant feeling of all. Susan had already muffled his moaning when she had sat on his face, her shaved pussy in his mouth, feeding him all of it. She was as wet as a pool on a rainy day and he loved the smell of her juices as they made their way across his lips and some of it on his mustache.

She smelt like tender flowers for all of the roughness which she exhibited, a steady pool of wetness. To imagine his cock in her pussy was not difficult to conjure as Lily gave the sensations as he would expect of her. Susan never took her pants off, Cameron just pushed it aside as he tongue fucked her, slapping her thick ass and flicking his tongue about her clitoris.

"God damn," he cried, when Lily deep throated his cock, gagging on the meat and slurping with the same move. It was a difficult and clumsy maneuver to get Lily's face out of the way when she deep-throat on it again, summoning his ejaculation quickly. Perhaps she knew what she was doing for when his cock spasmed quickly and he started to shoot his load, she did not take her mouth off it, instead, she pressed her face against his crotch so that he shot the load against the back of her throat.

"Good Lord!" he blurted, breaking a sweat after the ejaculation.

"Ah ah, not so fast," Susan said, realizing what had happened and she moved away from his face down to his dick, switching places with Lily.

Cameron's hips when numb for a few seconds when Susan licked on it, tingling the tip of his penis, where a stinging pleasurable sensation was most focused, to get the cum off it.

When Susan climbed his cock in a reverse cowgirl position, Cameron knew. The sensation was tighter and wetter. He reached his hands and touched on her butt once before the activity escalated. Her butt muscles twitched as she sat atop his laps, his cock halfway into her, ready to slowly give satisfaction to the rod and herself. Cameron sensed the twitch and before he could rub on it as his cognition instructed, Susan rode out of his hands. Cameron dumbed his senses to the thrill and diverted his attention to pleasing Lily.

Lily, unlike Susan, was a screamer when she received pleasure and Cameron gave loads of it with his tongue, lining the damp pussy with his tongue and licking the walls on the insides with such dedication that she creamed into his mouth whole screaming out her enjoyment, drowning the grunts of the other two in her presence.

Susan took her time sitting on the cock and fucking it halfway until she was creamy enough to lift herself into a squat, fucking the entire thing until Cameron regained sensations on his lower region. She held both his legs to keep her balance as she threw her ass against his cock, bouncing her butt against his crotch and making a creamy mess of his cock and the root of his shaft.

Lily stumbled off Cameron's face when she started to cum from his tongue work, vibrating unto her side as the waves of pure release hit her and screaming. Cameron moved Susan off him and rolled on his side to pick himself up. He stopped on his knees and pulled Lily closer, shoving his face into her pussy and licking on it to intensify her pleasures, working at it until she could take no more, pushing him away.

He turned around, managing both their attention in short bursts as he grabbed Susan to himself so that her butt faced him. He grabbed one of her cheeks and smiled when he thought of how thick her ass was. He slapped her ass and squeezed the cheek, pushing Susan's back so that it arched in the way that he wanted.

With one hand on her back and one hand on his cock, he eased himself into her from the back. As soon as he was all in, he placed the hands on her hips to keep her still, shortening the distance between each thrust. The image of a whitish paste on his cock incensed him sexually and he was in a frenzy when he started to whip, bounding and rebounding off her quickly as the whitish substance increased.

Susan held onto the floor as Cameron fucked with the strength of an ancient deity of lecherousness. It had been years since she has been so fucked that she came, but Cameron achieved that with his thrust upon the third minute of steady unbroken thrashing.

"I'm coming," she cried, bolting off his grip as she did. He followed her to the ground when she fell on her side, fucking her cum until her pussy from the force of the activity pushed his cock out as she gasped for oxygen.

Lily edged closer, recovered from her own ecstasy. She looked in his face and smiled, reaching her hand to his dangling cock and stroking it softly.

"You're something huh?" she said, still smiling.

Cameron reciprocated with a smile and silence, with pride as a soldier that had vanquished them both in a war of pleasures. Lily was back for more and Cameron was more than willing to oblige.

He held out his hands and she moved into it, as though he were a magnet and she was iron fillets. He held her head up and looked down into her eyes. The blank look on his face confused her and only when he smiled did she smile. He bent over her and kissed her as his fingers moved to her pussy, rubbing on her clitoris and scrubbing the strip of her pussy. He sensed she was wet and he stopped kissing her.

With both of them facing each other, Cameron held Lily and rolled onto his side to the left. He held her right leg over his hip and lowered his body so that her left leg was beneath him without touching even as he lay.

"Aww. Would you look at the lovers!" Susan quipped mockingly at the pose which the couple assumed. Neither of them paid her any mind to save the smile of acknowledgment which they shared.

Cameron slid into the tight pussy slowly and it purred, stuffed and stretched wide by his cock.

"Oh shit!" They both cried for different reasons. Lily's fingers on his back scratched a little as she tried to accommodate the full length of the cock which he pushed into her body.

Cameron breathed through a grunt as he attempted to thrust, Lily lowering her body to meet him halfway in the exercise. It was unbelievably satisfying so that Cameron had to throw his head backward to ease himself. Her pussy lubed his cock with a transparent coat and the thrusting became easier.

Lily's moaning was music, accompanying the sound of their slapping flesh against each other. If there was any doubt that Lily admired him, it was clear by the time Lily said those words at that moment.

"I love you, Cameron," she said, wrapping her arms around his neck as he stroked, pushing her ass up for deeper penetration.

Cameron was an easy man to please. The night had started slowly but surely it was ending with such a bang that even he could not have imagined it. He felt his toes curl and his legs go stiff as semen traveled the length of his shaft to the tip. He moved to pull out, but Lily held him to herself. A feeble attempt was put up to resist, however, it was too late.

Cameron lay on his side, overpowered by the second cumming than he had been by the first. All he wanted to do when he was spent was shut his eyes and dream endlessly of the evening.

My Friend's Mom

Since the third grade, Ben and Matt were inseparable. They shared each avocation, constantly had a class together and hung out with each other. Both these were a portion of the other's families to the point where their families were almost inseparable and undoubtedly best buddies.

Ben and Matt felt quite comfy discussing sexual topics like jerking off with each other. Matt had always understood how Ben had a thing for older girls. At the start of his senior year of high school, Ben felt an impulse to start masturbating to different elderly girls, not a porn star: Matt's mother. Tammy was in her mid-forties, had a pretty face, but was certainly obese. She was the most adorable woman to Ben. Ben, who wasn't one for big ladies, only felt the desire to pull up an image of her Facebook and stroke his youthful cock.

And so it started. Ben began to plan flirting with his very best friend's mother, who was constantly about hanging out with his mother or in her own home when Ben was with Matt.

A couple weeks following his first masturbating session into Tammy, Ben texted her. She was assisting his mother's plan to get a huge party for Ben's younger brother. He asked to her aid his mother since his father wasn't very involved with the celebration, and added that she looked really pretty that afternoon. She adored the compliments and Ben would sometimes write to her to let her know how he felt. His hugs when he watched her started including a little peck on the sidewalk, together with the impulse to attempt and touch her big butt. With that bum in mind, he snapped a photo of it, when together with her, he started his set of images to use.

On his next trip to her home, he sprinted upstairs while Matt was in the bathroom and jerked off to her underwear: the very first actual action of his tendency towards Tammy.

Weeks passed. Tammy and Ben started playing word games with each other over their phones. Conversation sparked from this and Ben utilized it as a chance to flirt with his MILF. Eventually, Ben decided to take the following step and say that he had the hots for her. The probable not sexually energetic mother of two was flattered. However, a couple of days afterwards, Ben decided to make things more clear.

When he left his cum in her large underwear, he was unsure whether she understood it was him. While over at her home for a party a night after, he left a huge load inside her panties and returned them to her drawer. Fourteen days later, they were texting about their phrase match when Tammy stated she'd been planning to sleep.

"Wait," Ben wrote, "Can I have a second?" Tammy responded she did along with Ben boldly apologizing about his semen departing. Together, with the adrenaline racing through his veins, he waited for her answer.

She accepted the apology and added, "That I was a little freaked out about the overstepping of boundaries in your role, but it was really flattering that trumps everything else."

Ben was amazed. This conservative mom had expressed that she'd been flattered that a handsome, tall, 18-year-old abandoned his dick's juices inside her large set of white cotton underwear. Tammy replicated to him that everything was OK and she had her discretion and didn't inform Ben's mom.

As Tammy said goodnight once more, Ben stopped the conversation with, "I owe you."

A couple of days later, Ben made strategies to spend time at Matt's and play some games on the XBOX. What he didn't understand was that Matt wasn't the one operating Matt's mobile phone. Ben drove to the Bome's home and was greeted at the door by Tammy.

He hugged her just like normal but her response was not the same. She reached her hands to Ben's jeans and grabbed his prick. "I wished to determine if I'd been working with a great one," she explained. Ben, stunned, was told, "Come upstairs. Matt's not home."

He followed Tammy upstairs, observing her chubby

ass swaying back and forth. The next thing he knew he was watching his best friend's mom took off the shirt she had on, unveiling her huge breasts. She motioned him to approach her on the mattress. "What I'd like is for you to place your handsome face right down on my pussy, then lick and fuck me until I cum," said the 47-year-old.

Ben stood there, too stunned to say anything else and obeyed.

His buddy's mother unveiled what had to be the best brown bush any girl might possess. He glided his tongue up and down her slit as she moaned and ran her hands through his thick brownish hair.

"Play with my breasts," she asked in bliss.

Since Ben worked his magic, she grabbed his cock and started stroking it up and down as her head leaned back. "Let me taste you baby," Tammy exclaimed while she watched the guy she saw grow up insert his penis between her handsome lips.

When Ben started to quiver, Tammy removed his penis and motioned with her eyes for Ben to start fucking her. Gradually, he entered her again, causing her to cried with delight.

Ben could not believe what was happening as he jammed his cock in and out of, essentially, his second mum. Eventually, she shrieked, suggesting to Ben it was time to unload the same cum that sat inside her underwear. They arrived together, finishing an unrivaled sexual encounter for both.

They went back into enjoying their iPhone games, not talking through the afternoon until ...

The Bomes and Wilks went to see a faculty together.

You're So Cute

I was sitting by myself at the bar drinking my rum and coke in Istanbul when I saw her make her way through the bar to me. She was the most alluring person I've ever laid eyes on. Large, jet-black, curly locks framed an angel's profile, and a deep-magenta sweater dress clung to her every curve. The fragrance of her intoxicating perfume flooded my nostrils and I felt fire slowly rising to my face as she sat beside me. She said "Rochelle?" "Yes" I purred, "and you must be Dominique" with a very hesitant accent. Paul, our mutual friend who set up the rendezvous, had not prepared me enough for her appearance.

"You're so cute," I whispered. Perhaps I shouldn't have been so frank in sharing my feelings, but her response to my comment gave me all the comfort I wanted. A light blush darkened her lips, and a quick intake of breath showed me she felt it too - that electric cursing current between us.

We spoke for the next hour or two, and knew each other a bit better. Then the drinks I had consumed along with the music's loud, pulsating beat led me to sway softly in my chair and my inhibitions started to fade. I've begun a long, romantic appraisal of my new friend. My gaze lingered on her big, firm breasts as I rubbed gently over my split lips with my index finger. When I imagined sucking and poking her puckered nipples, they actually started to respond, straining against her dress fabric. She has changed her position, squirming under my gaze's sheer need. I forced my eyes away from her luscious body to focus again on her exquisite facial features. Her deep blue eyes smoldered, her full and sensual lips enticing. Lightly putting my hand on her arm, I whispered, "Come home with me tonight." As soon as we reached my apartment's privacy and closed the door behind us, I put my hands on her face and pulled her mouth down to meet mine. Slipping my skilled tongue between her quivering lips, I sensed the sigh that had left her mouth, rather than being heard. I took her by the side, reaching down, and led her to my living room. I put her in my lap facing me, her hands on either side of mine, falling back into the softness of the plush sofa. This pose enabled me to see her magnificent body's every curve and orifice. Tugging on the bottom of her top, I lifted her up over her knees to expose wispy, white lace-cut satin. Kneading her thighs with the smooth, pliable skin, I sensed the stirrings of desire running through my own body.

"Take it off," I gasped, "I want to look at you." She shook her back, slowly pulling her dress up and over her shoulders, highlighting her stomach's sleek, taut muscles and the fullness of her heaving breasts. Instinctively grasping for them, as my fingertips kissed and tweaked her large pink nipples my palms caressed their sensitive undersides. I heard her whimper as I bent to taste one, and then the other, moving painfully slow, loving her reaction's intensity.

"Yeah," she moaned, "oh yes!" through the silk of her underwear I could smell her musky scent, and feel the heat of her desire. I held her face in my hands and kissed her fiercely, intensely, touching her inner essence, her breathing now becoming very ragged.

I managed to unbutton my blouse with slow and deliberate movements, rubbing her fingertips over my already hardened nipples as I did so. When she unsnapped my top and stared at my own full breasts when they spilled out into her cupped hands, a tiny moan escaped her mouth. Taking my lead, she drew tiny intense circles around my breasts and around them before finally reaching my enthusiastic nipples. Warm and soft, over my breasts and down the sensitive skin of my rib cage she blazed a trail of lust. The lightness of her touch and the warmth of her hands sent my entire body shivering with excitement and anticipation.

Eventually, she found her way to my form fitting denim waistband. I unconsciously raised my pelvis when I heard the button pop and felt her tugging at the zipper as a matter of urgency. My jeans fell down to my knees in one fluid movement, leaving me in my black lace panties which are now really dirty. She started a gentle exploration of my legs by putting her palms on the inside of my thighs, forcing them apart as she neared my throbbing cunt. She lowered her head to lick the shaking skin of my thighs and leaned her nose against the fabric of my underwear, tracing the shape of my swollen labia through the thin material with her tongue.

"I want you, my Lord," she groaned, stripping away the last barrier between her and my sopping wet cunt. I noticed her getting up from the couch, and my vision flickered. Stepping up, her hands went to her sexy underwear waistband.

"No," I moaned, "please let me." Ascending from the sofa, I kneeled in front of her and pressed my ear against her panties ' thin fabric. When I breathed into her musky scent, my mind reeled and rubbed my face back and forth across the wet material. I reached up and started to tug at her underwear, pushing them past the smooth whiteness of her knees, the strong muscles of her calves, gradually exposing to my hungry eyes her total nudity. In her elegance I have found.

I reached up to catch her slim waist and pulled her down to join me, both of us now wholly enthusiastic. I planted her feet on either side of my body spreading her legs wide. After reaching out, I put my hands behind her back, bringing her face to touch mine. My eyes captured her mouth. We passionately hugged. Our breathing has become more laborious. I reached down and cupped my palm over her wet cunt. With my thumb and index finger I pried softly open her pussy's swollen lips and inserted my middle finger through her flesh's sensitive folds. I felt a trembling beneath my touch's knowledge. Removing from our embrace, I gazed into her deep blue eyes.

"I want you to look at me," I hurriedly whispered, "I want to see you while you are cum." I gradually increased my finger speed and angled my thumb to apply pressure to her gorging clitoris.

"Is that what you want?" I chuckled. "Just tell me!" I commanded.

"Yeah... that's it... oh, yeah, yeah," she screamed when I inserted another digit and her hips started buckling my side. Shoving my nails into the hilt, I moved them back and forth quickly, pounding her at a furious pace. Her head snapped around and it coaxed me even further with her guttural screams.

"Cum for me," I ordered, "let everything go." Now, bracing her hands against the cement, she raised her pelvis and thrashed desperately at my hand as she gasped and wailed in ecstasy. She was really the most beautiful creature I'd ever looked at.

She pulled herself up to look at me as her breathing began to subside. She bent forward, put her arms around my waist, and rested her head on my chest after a few lengthy moments of merely looking into one another's eyes. "This is only my beautiful beginning," I whispered, putting my arms around her quivering body and pulling her tighter to me, "only the beginning..."

The Sexy MILFs First Time Anal Sex

We all know how life can be sometimes but recently I have gotten it in double doses. I'm a single mom of two kids who struggles to get through a normal day with my sanity intact, so why not add a busted sink to the mix just to push me over the edge? It was probably the worst time for a plumbing problem in the history of the world. That would be my vote anyway. Just when I thought things couldn't get any worse, the bill was outrageous and I was out of options. Right about that time when I was ready to give up, something happened with the young plumber that shocked me to my core in a very good way.

"That will be four-hundred and fifty-six dollars and ninety-three cents ma'am."

I nearly dropped my glass of water. Somehow the young man said it with a straight face which just added to my misery. All I could do was stare at him in wonder at how greatly he overestimated my ability to take a joke. At one time I could have taken a joke pretty well but those days were few and far between now as a single mom with two kids on a salary that would make a first year teacher feel like the owner of Trump Towers. I didn't know what to do so I told him to wait just a moment while I went to get the money and walked into the bedroom.

This was bad, I told myself – as if I didn't know. I had missed half a day of work already and now this stud thinks I have nearly five-hundred dollars stuffed in my sock drawer. He couldn't be more wrong. Maybe I could just appeal to his better nature and he would tell me the real, much lower price. Heck, I didn't even have a credit card with that much room on it but he had already fixed the sink; not that I would have been able to not get the thing fixed. Washing dishes in the bathtub just makes me want to cry and we cannot have that.

A check of the clock on the bedroom wall showed that I still had a few hours before I needed to pick up Jackson and Rayleigh from school but that still didn't help my situation. Maybe I could rob a bank in that amount of time. They'd just think I was joking and I no more own a weapon than I know how to fire one.

For the first time, I began to rethink my having turned down an offer to dance at night at a local strip club. It wasn't exactly a hard decision except for the simple fact that a longtime friend of mine was the owner of the club that offered. And sure, I'm in my mid-thirties but I stay in top physical condition by doing – well not much.

I have naturally high metabolism and just keeping a decent amount of activity in my daily routine keeps me golden.

When he offered me the job dancing, he said that he had never seen a guy who wouldn't want to see my body on display up there and that he would make sure nobody mistreated me. In spite of the fact that I felt like he was marginally telling the truth, I figured he probably said something similar to all the girls, so I turned him down. With the richest plumber on the planet waiting patiently on my ship to come in across the house, I really wished I had at least agreed to tend the bar for him.

While I was thinking back and hoping the plumber would just decide to leave without being paid, I also began to relive some of the happenings in life that had brought me to that point. The biggest mistake I ever made also happened to be the same thing that brought my biggest blessings. Jacob was my high school sweetheart. We went to the prom and every other dance as well as all of the parties together before hanging out all through college as well. Shortly after college we were married and all I needed for my dreams to come true was a white picket fence and a few kids.

Dreams don't always come true though and that was

the case with mine. Jacob turned out to be something of a jerk once I started living in the same house with him. It was almost like he flipped a switch on the week after we said our vows and decided to be a piss head for the rest of his life. On top of mistreating me for a while, he also refused to give me children which was another sudden change from our dating years. Eventually, just before everything fell apart, I convinced him to try children just for the sake of saving the marriage. That worked for us about as well as ordering a gourmet meal from the fast food joint down the street.

I'll never regret Jack and Rayleigh. They are my heart. Every other part of the marriage was a joke and a disappointment that I honestly could have done without. The two of them are in elementary school now and are doing well. I had planned to home-school them because I hate the way organized school is handled but that choice was taken out of my hands by my situation and I can't afford private education by a long shot. Luckily we found a good school in the district and they are flourishing.

That morning when they went off to school, the sink began to gush water all over the kitchen floor. My Dad taught me well enough to know how to turn the water off so I did that under the counter and took the kids to the bus stop before calling work and telling them I had a plumbing emergency to deal with. Dinner would need to be ready in time for a good night sleep for all three of us and I needed the kitchen sink for that because my dishwasher hasn't worked in a long while. All of which brings me to the present time, with the stubbornly handsome young plumber propping on the kitchen counter, patiently waiting on me to pay him.

Maybe I could just jump out the window.

"Miss? Have you found your payment yet? I have a few other jobs to get to, not to rush you though. I was just wondering."

Miss. Why does he have to call me Miss and ma'am? I'm not that old, maybe ten years or so older than him. He could still be attracted to me. I found myself attracted to him well enough. Ah, he probably had a hot college girlfriend a few years younger than him and thought of me as being like his aunt's age or something. Finally, I figured the longer I hid in the other room the more stupid he would probably think I was so I headed towards the door.

When I opened it the edge of the door hit my hand just hard enough to knock the water glass out of my grasp. It fell harmlessly to the carpet but not before it dumped half of the glass on my shirt. "Damn-it!" I said in frustration.

"Ma'am?"

"Nothing!" To myself I added, Stop calling me ma'am! "I'll be right there!" I yelled because I was far too frustrated to pretend I was fine. With few other options I just pulled the wet blouse off and threw it to the floor. It left me in my skimpy undershirt that was also a little wet. Hopefully it wouldn't look too strange since I was barefoot with comfy around-the-house pants on.

The smile I plastered onto my face was obvious false when I finally made it out of the room and walked towards the kitchen. He stood up straight and looked straight at my undershirt as if in shock. "Yeah," I sighed and ran my hand through my long brown hair, "Dumped a cup of water on myself just to make sure I was still awake. Look, I can't afford that. I'm sorry, I really thought it wouldn't be that much. I even searched the internet for quotes and most of them weren't anywhere close to that much. I don't know what to do."

He finally peeled his eyes from my shirt and said, "Emergency."

"What?" I asked confused.

Shaking his head he said, "Um, you identified it as an emergency so the cost went way up."

"That's stupid."

"That's plumbing business ma'am," he said which drew

a look of pure hatred from me. "Be glad you didn't call in the middle of the night. It wouldn't have been that bad but the problem with the sink also meant I had to fix and replace some of the plumbing to the dishwasher."

I sighed, "The dishwasher? It hasn't worked in years. I only wanted the sink to work. God, it wasn't that big of an emergency. You have to help me out somehow."

He thumbed his pants and shrugged, "It might get me in trouble ma..."

"If you call me ma'am again I'm going to slap the taste out of your mouth!" I said with a finger pointed in his face.

His head pulled back slightly, he put his hands up, "I'm sorry, I always get nervous around hot women so I was trying to be polite. It might get me in trouble but I will see what I can do. Let me go out to my truck and call my boss. It's the least I can do since it really wasn't that difficult of a fix."

I didn't hear a lot of what he said after that because I was stuck on him saying I was hot. Here I was thinking he saw me as an older washed up woman and that wasn't true at all. Watching him go, I noticed the tightness of his jeans and began to wish he showed a little more than simple plumber's crack. Standing out at his truck he was pretty animated as he spoke. I only caught a few words he said but it looked like he was really trying to argue my case. Finally he looked at his phone and pressed the screen before throwing it into the truck and slamming the door.

Quickly I scooted back across towards the kitchen and started thumbing through the old napkin holder where my credit cards were. If the price came down far enough I could put it on one of them but I had to find the damn thing. At least it gave me something to do so he might not know I was watching him the entire time he was gone. He was standing there with his thumbs in his pockets again with a little bit of a red tint to his cheeks. I figured that was from his frustration at the end of the conversation. Finally I realized he was staring at me as if he didn't know what to say. I looked up at him with more admiration than I had before and said, "My name is Hannah."

"Hannah," he said, "My stupid fucking boss only will let me take a hundred off of the price. He said something about breaking the payments up but that's stupid. Look," he sighed, "How much can you afford?"

I winced, "One-fifty? Maybe one-sixty."

With a stiff nod he said, "That will work. I can just copy down the card information and then I'll be on my way.

I'm sorry about this Hannah. I tried to talk him down farther but he is a rich dip-shit and doesn't like people. Oh, please excuse my language."

A smile forced its way to my face at what he was saying. "I know you tried. Thank you but what about the rest of the money? Will you get fired?"

"Nah," he waved a hand towards me, "I'll pay the rest of it out of my own pocket if I have to. It's not right to take advantage of you like that. Just pay what you can and I'll add the rest and say you broke up the payment between two different cards or something."

"You'd do that for me?"

His frustration was still visible as he shrugged, "Yeah, why not. Good people deserve to have good things happen to them now and then."

"I agree with that much." Now I was walking towards him with pure infatuation visible in my manner, "It's been a long time since anyone did something that nice for me. How could I ever repay you?"

"Forget about it," he said with a smile which suggested he noticed the look on my face. "Doing something nice for a beautiful woman is reward enough by itself."

"Maybe it is," I said now within a step of him and looking him over slowly, "Or maybe it's not. I think I have to give you a kiss on the cheek at least for being my hero. The hero always gets a kiss after all." I ran my hand up his stiff and strong chest. He began to get a little nervous in the way he stood and said that was fine if I wanted to. My hand cupped behind his neck and pulled his face down a little towards mine. He turned his cheek towards my lips but instead I grabbed his face with my other hand and twisted his lips towards mine so that my kiss slammed against his lips directly.

At first he pulled back but I went with him and he quickly began to return the kiss. It grew from an awkward kiss to a passionate lip to lip kiss and then to a fully passionate kiss as he grabbed my neck and met my need with his own. We were lost there in the moment for I don't know how long before we both stopped but didn't pull away. My eyes searched his handsome features as his searched mine and I said, "Maybe the hero gets more than just a kiss." Our lips met once again and this time it felt like long lost lovers seeing each other again after years apart as we held each other close.

When our lips parted again he looked down and said, "I don't want to take..."

"....advantage of me. I know." I kissed him quickly as I ran my fingers through his hair, "But that's a problem."

"It is?"

"Yes," I said, "Because that is exactly what I want you to do."

Those words seem to hang in the slim space between us for a few moments as he stared at me and me back at him. I wondered what he would do. Clearly he wanted me, was more enamored with me than I had imagined when I first admired his stride into the kitchen that morning. The small hope growing inside me that he would take me in his arms and move me into the bedroom wound up a little too much of a fairytale however.

When he took me, he didn't move me anywhere. Instead he started by pulling his shirt off, revealing his thin but strong upper body. Before I could follow suit and remove mine he did it for me, grasping the bottom of the shirt and pulling it off over my head as I lifted my arms to make it easy. I removed my bra so quickly that it was on the ground before his chest touched mine as he embraced and kissed me again.

He lifted me in arms that felt stronger or maybe filled with the power of desire as he spun me around and sat me on the counter. His fingers grabbed the waist of my pants and pulled them downward. I planted my palms on the counter and lifted my backside as he pulled not only my pants but my panties down and off over my feet. I smiled and threw my head back as the cold counter on my butt and the brush of his rough fingers on my thighs sent chills all over my body.

It had been so long since somebody looked at me the way he was looking at me when he tossed my panties to the floor and rose back towards me that I actually giggled. By then he was fully into the flow of the moment and was coming for me but I surprised him by pushing off of the counter and standing in front of him as I slowly unbuckled his jeans and unbuttoned his jeans. As I dragged his jeans downward, his boxers came with it all the way to the floor, returning the favor for what he had just done to me. I smiled up at him mischievously as I knelt down to the floor, "How do you like it?"

He groaned towards the ceiling as my hands ran over his swollen shaft, "Holy shit you're hot."

"I know," winking I reached towards the tip with my tongue, teasing him. I would have been lying or being sarcastic if I had suggested that I thought I was hot only an hour before but right then I felt more attractive than I had in a decade of losers in bars and a deadbeat husband. There wasn't a model walking any runway in the world with more confidence than me as I kissed the end of his throbbing cock. My fingers were working him over right as I squeezed the base with one hand and teased his balls with the other. I could tell by his body language, his groans and the way his cock was growing even more tight and hard that I was pushing all the right buttons so I didn't stop.

Refusing to close my eyes or break eye contact with him for more than a second or two, I ran my lips along the end of his shaft and sucked hard as I lifted back off. He was easily the biggest I had ever done that with but then I didn't just go down on anyone. This guy was something special though. I could feel it. As I ran my mouth along his cock I could feel the throbbing and paid close attention so that I didn't push him too close to the edge of a climax. He was young enough to probably be able to go more than once but I didn't dare risk it.

When his hips began to tense up, I pulled off of him and stood up, running my nails over his chest slowly. Lost to the moment, I wiped a little bit of spittle from the edge of my mouth and backed up with a sultry look in my eyes before hopping up onto the edge of the kitchen counter. After spreading my thighs open I glared at him with a look of longing, "You're turn."

He didn't hesitate for a fraction of a second, moving in and scooping my butt into his hands, lifting my eager pussy to his mouth. I thought he was going to get started right away and wanted nothing more but instead he licked along the edge of my pussy and then kissed down my inner thigh. Slowly he teased downward towards my knee before moving to the other thigh and kissing his way back upwards. I lifted my hips upwards towards him as my moans begged him to get started.

For a second he skipped over my pussy and started towards the other thigh but I couldn't take it anymore. My hands left the counter, dropping me to the counter, and I grabbed the back of his head to force him to my pussy. He didn't fight it or try and tease me more, instead dropping his tongue directly into my damp slit and releasing his hold on my hips so that he could use his hands and fingers. One hand went directly to my breasts where his thumb and forefinger squeezed and twirled my nipples expertly. I slid further down so that my back was now completely resting on the counter with my knees up and spread out to the side and ran one hand through my hair while keeping the other on the back of his head. I wanted him to keep going, needed him badly to keep going.

With his other hand he reached between my legs and began to add to my pleasure by teasing my clit. Then he switched and licked my clit, flicking it one way and the other while his finger drove into my pussy wonderfully. Everything might feel better in the moment but I was certain that nothing had ever been done to me that felt as good as what he was doing right then. I began to moan loudly as he continued to work over my pussy and felt an orgasm building as my hand moved from my hair to squeeze the breast he wasn't giving direct attention to.

It could have gone on forever and I would have been okay with it but quickly he switched to a standing position and pulled my body forward into his grasp. I wrapped my arms and legs around him and buried my lips into his neck, eagerly awaiting the blessed inevitable. Slowly he lowered me down to his shaft and I clung tightly to him with my eyes closed as he eased inside of me. His pace quickened immediately as he began driving into me. He filled me better than anyone ever had and I felt almost like it was my first time all over again, only much better.

Our hips were clashing together as the first orgasm broke over me and I sank back away from him, allowing his strong grasp alone to keep me from falling to the floor. It only served to make him feel that much better inside of me and another more powerful orgasm immediately crashed over me. I lost track of all time, worry and any need other than my need for him. He moved me around the kitchen into different embraces for a few minutes until I finally thought he was going to finish.

An orgasm was building inside of me and couldn't be held back once his pace quickened even more. My body was still gyrating around as his grunts grew louder and I knew he was going to cum. I pointed at my chest and he pulled out and blew his huge load all over my chest. He sat me on the counter and I rested back against the cabinet door. When my eyes slowly fluttered open, he was standing there looking at me with the same look of need in his eyes and I noticed his erection was still strong.

He moved forward and dug his fingers into my butt with one of them moving towards my crack and whispered, "Have you ever?"

With his fingers pulling at my butt cheeks I knew exactly what he meant. I had never even considered anal with anyone. It was always something that I didn't trust anyone to do or was never into someone enough to try. I glared at him with a playful look my mirror hasn't seen in over a decade, biting my pinky nail in the corner of my mouth, "First time for everything..."

With zero hesitation he dragged me off of the counter, lifting me enough so that the corner didn't hurt me on the way down. I groaned as he turned me around and bent myself over the counter with my feet spread apart. At first he worked on me with his fingers, dragging at my cheeks and inserting his thumb into me anally. It was nothing I had ever felt before but it wasn't taking me long to get into it as I grasped and squeezed my breasts.

He reached around to my pussy and dug his fingers inside of me. I moaned loudly as he then moved my own juices around to my anus and then started to push his shaft inside. At first I was silent. My eyes were clamped closed tightly. This didn't just feel like another first time, it was the very first time. Quickly a little pain gave way to a little pleasure.

His shaft moved in and then out before pushing slowly back in a little farther. My head lolled back as he stretched me with each slow thrust. He knew exactly what he was doing and as I started to like it more, he increased his pace and power. Every time he entered me and stretched me that much more, I thought I was going to have another blast of orgasmic bliss wash over me. The feeling was so huge and so new that I can't even put it into words that would do it justice.

Within a few minutes he began pushing inside of me faster and harder and my tight moans and groans turned into louder yelps of pleasure. Part of me wanted to order him to go harder and deeper but instead I just enjoyed groaning loudly as he showed me what anal sex was supposed to be and I loved every second of it. Just when I thought it couldn't feel any better, he reached one of his hands around and began fingering my pussy and pussy lips again.

My hands instantly were planted on the counter and my back arched as the biggest orgasm yet came over me so hard that my knees buckled. I was able to stay on my feet as he kept driving into me. It was so wonderful that I never wanted it to end. The way he started breathing and grunting harder suggested that I wouldn't be so lucky however so I told him to go harder and faster.

He was nearly yelling as he finished with a thunderous climax all over my backside and my final orgasm hit at nearly the same time. For a while I propped on the counter and he moved back to rest against the counter behind me. I don't know how long we rested there in silence. I turned around to face him and he smiled as he pulled his jeans back on.

"Hannah, that was the most amazing thing I've ever done."

I grinned, "I've had better." There was a slight frown on his face before I moved to place my hand on his chest and whispered, "Just kidding. You're such a stud I didn't want it to end."

"I was wondering," he shrugged, "Maybe you needed some help around the house now and then? I could give you my cell number and you can just call me direct or text or something. I'd love to," he heaved a breath and smiled, "Hell, I want to do that again."

"You're a great guy and I wouldn't pass up the chance to have some help now and then. I think the second bathroom needs some work," I grinned. "I think we can make time for another plumbing emergency."

He laughed, "Good to hear."

As he wrote his number down and we both got dressed, I realized that I didn't even know his name. It was probably for the best. Whenever I texted him I would probably just ask for plumbing help and see if he knew who I was. The best lover I had ever had was a plumber I didn't even know, who was ten years younger than me. Something about that, a lot of something about it in fact, was making me want him again before he backed out of the driveway. I forced myself to behave if only for a few days before I started teasing another encounter. He was just as eager as I was to get together again.

Her Halloween Plans

"What a sensational night that was!" Every time Melissa recalled those night-time experiences, she felt enchanted. A day before the party, when Melissa discussed with Clara about her Halloween plans, she felt somewhat heartbroken due to her recent breakup. But Clara said: "Darling! No party is a party without you. And, you can always retake a night long sleep, but can never relive a fun-filled night long thrilling party, can you?" And thus, with her compelling charm and majestic charisma, Clara convinced Melissa to attend her party. She couldn't say no. As Melissa didn't have any special dress, Clara allowed her to borrow one of hers. That was so generous of her! Besides, she was a bit childish in her entertainment ideas. Hence, requested her fellow partisans to dress up like some comic or movie characters. And, in due time, there Melissa was enjoying Clara's party dressed up as "the Harley Quinn"!!

In fact, Clara felt more insane in her appearance because she was unaware of the fact that how she would be accepted. It had a short white mini shirt, with white inflated shoulders, followed by a normal white collar. But the mini shirt was so low cut and opened that it exposed her busty cleavage. Moreover, the single ponytail hairstyle proclaimed her attractive appearance as it resembled the crown of some insane villainous goddess. The exposure of her radiant skin around her navel and curvy statuesque body only coupled her ravishing outlook. She looked more of a psychotic punk rocker in her mini skirt. Furthermore, Melissa wore high heeled boots in red and purple shades and a black fishnet stocking that provided a classy touch to her get-up. "Oh, my God! I didn't know how I looked," Melissa wondered several times before entering the party. "Probably, you're in search of your Joker. Ha-ha," Clara teased Melissa in between, several times. Despite being surprised at her own boldness, she unexpectedly received plenty of compliments and attention. And that splendid Halloween party brought her to life once again.

When the party started it was totally a magical environment at Clara's residence. Melissa, though the center of attraction in the party, and she did find herself in a little bit awkward situation amongst other guests. The moon resembled the glittering disco ball and shone all throughout the night. The glowing, glittering and shimmering lighting decorations only vibrated and enhanced the lively party atmosphere of the room which held the main event. Moreover, with the DJ playing the latest hit songs and uninterrupted supply of drinks, it just provided a splendid and joyful welcome to the guests. Gradually, the awkwardness and edginess in Melissa's mind and heart faded away and he started to feel the beat. After a few drinks, she was so relaxed that she even posed for some pictures with the fellow party attendees. "Oh, my God! They were all crazy to feel my body!" Melissa wondered

It was hard for Melissa to divert her attention from a guy who dressed like the JOKER in "The Dark Knight" movie. Clara had teased Melissa before saying, "As you're dressed up like "Harley Quinn", probably you're in search of your "Joker". And that came back rocking her senses for a moment when she finally found her JOKER. Undoubtedly, he received considerable applause from the party attendees for his funny behavior and magic tricks. Like the movie character, he wore the green colored jacket. His magnificently elegant costume was further accompanied by a stunning printed tie. But, the best awe-inspiring part of his costume was the hexagon patterned printed shirt that was a completely new look for everyone. Surprisingly, he was quite flirty with Melissa. He introduced himself as Dominic Lefebvre, but Melissa preferred to call him Dom. Enormously built like a masculine bodybuilder, he was a mixed martial arts trainer and was of French origin. Besides, he was kind of hilarious with his poor jokes that made Melissa laugh aloud, which caught Clara's eyes and she frequently winked at her. When he asked her to dance with him, Melissa was really blushing and hesitant.

Dom sternly enquired: "What frightens my Harley Quinn?"

Melissa mumbled: "I'm not sure. Probably, it's that I haven't danced in years."

He probed again: "Well, someone correctly quoted that the shortcut to happiness is dancing."

His animated words and that chuckle on his face streamed electrifying chills through her spines. Was he toying with her mind? Did he know something about her? Probably, a perfect blend of wine and the party music intoxicated Melissa. She found him too irresistible. Soon enough, she felt excited again to shake her hips and legs. But she didn't know what was holding her back.

Probing further, he hissed into her ears: "What are you thinking Harley?" and Melissa felt his warm breath on her soft skin. All of a sudden she could hear her heart pounding a thousand times. Also, she sensed him deeply inhaling the fragrance of her tempting perfume.

In return, Melissa could only mumble: "I'm not sure."

Instantaneously he whispered: "Nobody puts my Quinn in the corner."

Instead of whispering into her ears, Melissa felt like he spoke to her soul. Perhaps, Venus and Aphrodite had other plans for her. And finally, she had to surrender to his addictive demands and her hidden wishes. Melissa replied: "Okay, I won't just dance with you. Let me dance with you on the edge, and then I'm going to push you off and then jump with you with a smile on my face."

She hadn't shaken her hips and legs in... years or was it that she was still nervous to rock the dance floor with him. But, when Dom held Melissa's hands, it was so electrifying and surprisingly, her anxiety receded behind the walls of her desires. Perhaps, she was waiting patiently for his touch; her hunger was once again inflamed to be desired. Everyone praised their talents and they felt like college lovebirds dating together. But Melissa thought for a moment, that being dressed like a temptress, and dancing with an enormous six and a half feet tall European hunk, probably stimulated their audiences' fascination.

With Dominic holding Melissa's hands and always around her, she felt so happy, relaxed and comfortable. When the attendees started leaving after dinner, they sneaked into a lonely area of Clara's house just to spend time together. But Melissa was too afraid to break the ice. But Dominic took the initiative and kissed her lips. She didn't feel strange; rather it felt so natural and positively electric. Then, there they were, standing alone on the terrace. He was appreciating her ponytail hairstyle when he tenderly grabbed her hair. Tilting her head back, he leaned forward and kissed her. Wow! Melissa felt chills and thrills shaking her spines. She didn't know anything about him. But, she realized when he kissed her again, she became alive and her whole world changed gloriously. It dazzled her senses arousing the lush erotica buried deep inside her heart. Perhaps, both the heaven and the hell descended into her brains and conquered her own secret world.

Melissa stood there with her head tilted back, kissing Dominic deeply with their tongues twisted together. As she continued her ecstatic journey, Melissa felt her sensations pulsating inside her. Wrapping her arms around him, she dragged him close while he wandered his hands down her back and tightly cupped her ass. When he wandered his fingers in between her legs, Melissa shook in savage lust and moaned out loud. And, they realized that they needed more privacy. Dominic investigated their surroundings; Melissa hoped and was relieved to discover that no one was watching them. To her sheer surprise, he was very much aware of Clara's house and led the way to the basement. Unbelievably, Melissa followed his footsteps without any hesitation.

As soon as they entered the basement, Dominic locked the door. Melissa sensed what was supposed to happen as Melissa was waiting for her man to enkindle the passionate lust and inflame her savage wants; Melissa blushed to see Dominic and stating, "How's my slut doing for the night?"

Melissa was absolutely stupefied at the lecherous comment of Dominic especially when her they had just become so intimate. Melissa shushed and seductively twisted herself on the couch where she settled provoking Dominic's arousal. Melissa gestured Dominic to have his seat beside her on the couch. The potent stud was exhibiting his enormous swelling muscles.

Melissa felt her heart beating like drums, her entire body shuddering with excitement when she wondered how this hunk man would look naked and bare; she always had a taste for hunk men. Her ex-husband had a pleasant looking body for his age however he was no muscle god like Dominic. As time passed, Melissa allowed her wild lust to corrupt her spirit and licked her lips seductively to tempt Dominic more. Her mind was flooded with sinful thoughts of how she was going to fly the highest peaks of lust with her lover.

Her line of reasoning was cut when Dominic unexpectedly jumped on her and kissed her feverishly on the fleshy lips. Her first response was an absolute shock, but afterward, she melted like wax in the amorous warm embrace of her lover, Dominic. He seemed to devour her luscious lips with his huge thick lips. His course tongue invaded her juicy mouth to meet with her soft tongue and swap saliva.

Dominic was a true lion as he was always, and he was ravishing Melissa's lush framework. His hands were all over her body, squeezing her succulent bosoms with full force that drove her to the point of excruciating agony, pressing and slapping on her juicy pussy. But then again, Melissa lived the blend of pain and pleasure. He always yearned for her man to be rough and hard with her.

The pressure, the powerful sexual ministrations and the tempting imagination of his naked body on her were a lot for her. In two minutes, Melissa was shivering in lecherous wants. She found herself completely topless with brawny lover sucking voraciously at her perky nipples, kneading them, chewing them, licking them while his hands were mauling her enormous bosoms.

Melissa had never given anybody a chance to ravage her like that. Her ex-husband was so gentle on her unlike this bull ravishing her. Pushing under her mini skirt, Dominic obliged the Melissa to take it off and soon the panties followed.

There she was, a recently divorced woman, absolutely stripped on the couch with a brawny stud, being sexually utilized by a man who wasn't even her husband. Dominic was a specialist in dealing with married women and MILFs who had decent, loving and caring husbands. He always knew how to liberate the whore inside them; the true woman that their decent, loving husbands did not know even existed. That was the charisma by which he had wished to penetrate Melissa.

Taking his left hand, Dominic grabbed Melissa's moistening pussy and started to play with it and squeeze on it. A deep lustful groan escaped Melissa's mouth. These were stimulating sensations that she had always ached and craved to experience. Without further delay, Melissa felt one finger penetrating her sacred chamber as one of her perky nipples was all the while being chomped, kneaded and sucked voraciously by Dominic.

She bounced a little pleasurable excitement on the couch and snaked her hands on his huge muscular forearm desperately attempting to push it away. Instead, Dominic shoved his finger further into the divorced lady's pussy. Melissa felt her juices streaming and she was not able to resist any further the brutal ministrations of her lover. She let him keep on fingering her.

Melissa was enjoying her ecstatic pleasure rides with her lover Dominic. Removing his pants, Dominic remained in his messy shirt while being totally stripped starting from the waist. Before he came to grab her, Dominic removed his boxers. This way it is quicker. Dominic sensed that Melissa was acting like a bitch in heat and cunt was well lubed from her own juices so he lifted her up in his masculine arms and let her down on his huge erect pole. When the precum covered, the cock head of the potent stud touched Melissa's cunt lips, a jolt of electricity coupled with a chilling flow shot through her entire body from her toes to her head.

Moaning a little louder as she was brought down on Dominic's huge fuck pole, Melissa felt her cunt being dilated. This was the first time she had experienced such a wild feeling with anybody. She had never experienced this feeling with her ex-husband. Gradually, the bitch in heat sunk on the big hardened erection until she was completely impaled on the masculine stud's monster. Melissa clutched the brawny broad shoulders of Dominic impaling her on his hardened manhood. She was consumed with overwhelming wants, savage lust and wild desires; she was so consumed and corrupted that only a hunk like Dominic could put out the fire in her burning body. Hence, right now, she wasn't thinking straight, all her psychological power was concentrated in her cunt on the mammoth pussy breaker conquering her worldly senses. As Melissa raised and lowered herself on the potent shaft, her succulent bosoms jiggled and loud sultry groans escaped from her throat as if she were being exorcised. Melissa shut her eyes as the delightful ecstasy of pain and pleasure in her overstretched cunt overwhelmed her. "Is this how a woman should feel when she is filled to the brim with a masculine hunk's potent shaft?" Melissa wondered in her own euphoric delight. "Why do I miss all these stimulating pleasures with my ex-husband and only experiencing them with Dominic?" Melissa's amorous mind was crowded with all sorts of illicit questions. She was unable to make decisions; but she certainly knew something:: The lustful delights she was experiencing, was from another man, Dominic, her most recent ardent lover who made her sit on a cloud high above.

Melissa felt the electrifying delight as she was fed by Dominic's 8 inch fuck pole. Even if she added up all the love nights with her ex-husband in five years of her unsuccessful marriage, her ex-husband was no match for this potent hunk who always drove her insane and gave her wings to fly the ecstatic pleasures of the highest heavens.

Dominic, all of a sudden grabbed Melissa by her waist and she watched his muscles flexing as he moved her faster up and down on his throbbing erection. If anybody had ventured into the room discreetly, definitely, they would consider Melissa to be a whore pleasing the potent stud in the cellar. But, Melissa didn't care for the world then. Her world was Dominic, shoving his potent shaft in her yearning pussy vigorously and using her as a fuck toy. Her lustful moans became more intense and Melissa muffled herself with her mouth not to make their presence felt by other men still enjoying the after party in the other room, as Dominic's gigantic erection filled her totally.

"I'm going to fuck you hard slut? I'm going to make that pussy ache so that when you remember tomorrow, you can recall who did this to you." Dominic breathed in Melissa's ears, sending chills of ecstasy down her spine.

"Oh," Melissa's voice was husky. "Fuck me hard. Hurt my pussy"

"You're a slut waiting to be freed!" Dominic groaned.

Moreover, Dominic started biting feverishly the huge milk buckets of the bitch in heat. He was completely consumed by his overpowering lust for this fuck toy. What's more, whenever the thought of ravishing a slut like Melissa crossed his mind, his manhood throbbed harder. He was passionately aroused by the act of taking this priceless bitch in the party, "Harley Quinn" aka Melissa.

After 45 minutes of riding the gigantic erection, Melissa was delirious; she had already climaxed multiple times and the stud still under her was continuing fucking her brains out.

Investigating his eyes, Melissa discovered an animalistic lust as Dominic gritted his teeth bellowed. Soon she sensed cock head of the shaft ramming her womanhood expand and the balls boiling under her married pussy. Stream after stream of intense hot cum burned her womb and cervix. She yelled at the electrifying sensation shuddering like a dry leaf as her hands were unable to muffle her groans. Dominic violated her juicy lips kissing her in lust while she was kissing him back in gratitude for the amorous delight, he had given her.

After they had finished, surges of white cum spilled out of the slut's freshly fucked womanhood and her bosoms were marked with love bites from the potent stud.

After a few minutes, they heard someone's footsteps, they got alarmed and got dressed quickly making their way into the noise and hubbub of the after party. Probably, they had gone missing for almost one hour and a half.

A jubilant Clara exclaimed: "Well! Well! I think this Halloween party ended up extremely thrilling for Harley Quinn and her Joker. I hope you were not bored!" Clara's sarcasm stupefied Melissa beyond limitations and she was fortunate that Dominic rose up to the occasion and answered sternly: "How can a party be so boring when you have such an attractive temptation as the show's topper?" Clara winked her eyes and grinned which made Melissa conclude that she probably knew what could have possibly cooked in between them. Risking nothing further, Melissa thought to depart from the party. Besides, she was really feeling tired. Dominic and Melissa exchanged numbers, decided to meet sometime soon. It was too horny and taboo that at that moment she felt his cum oozing out of her freshly fucked cunt and making its way through the fishnet stocking.

Every time Melissa thought about her Halloween experience, she still couldn't believe what she had experienced. But Dominic was worthy of a man, so was she. Will she hear from him soon?

The Swingers Club

I met a young tender angel "Cat" in 2007 in a nightclub, her asking me for a light. She was 22 and I was 23. She was absolutely stunning, red hair, slim, but with gorgeous d cup breasts and a firm ass. We talked for hours before she asked if I was going to kiss her. She came back to mine with some friends and I cooked her a late night meal, which she has since told me had swung it for me. She stayed the night and hasn't been out of my life since.

2 years later, I built up the courage to ask her to marry me and the following year we tied the knot. I felt and still feel completely loved and secure with her. I don't think I could ever love a person more.

Our sex life started great, as many relationships do, but Cat was special. She was the first girl I'd been with that happily swallowed me cum, taken me in her ass as well as playing with my ass. But unlike previous relationships, the sex didn't peter out to once every few weeks and I've never felt from her that I'm not wanted. I guess her sex drive is nearly as high as mine.

My previous relationship ended badly, with the revelation that she had been cheating on me with countless people. Obviously, I was hurt and ended the relationship due to the betrayal, but didn't feel ill will towards her.

Around this time, I started to think more about the idea of watching it happen, the person I loved fucking in front of me. I was also watching a lot of interracial porn and for some reason, found the contrast against white skin, strong muscular physique and often large cocks of black men portrayed in porn a huge turn on.

I also became fascinated with cum and developed a fetish for the idea of being forced to taste and eat cum from my dominant partner.

As you can probably tell, I tend to be more submissive in nature. I can play the part of being more dominant and have done so many times with Cat, but it doesn't come naturally to me. Cat is also more submissive, but she is great at taking control when she is in the mood.

Bringing up my fantasies has been challenging for me due to fear of Cat being disgusted by the idea or thinking less of me.

Early on in our relationship, when we were in the heat of the moment, I started talking dirty to Cat about cumming all over her and her being covered in cum by lots of different cocks. I think it was a bit too much, too fast, as she started to say things like I don't think that would be right. I backed off.

On our honeymoon, one drunken night, I confessed my fetish for cum and my desire for her to dominate me and force me to eat cum from her. Like most men though, the desire disappeared after I came, and not wanting to scare her off right after our marriage, didn't go as far to say I'd like her to force me to eat someone else's cum from her.

I had seen a few cum eating instruction videos online that instructed to freeze cum before eating. I had no real desire to do this on my own, but Cat agreed to try it.

We tried this a few times, but didn't really do it for either of us. It was uncomfortable for her to put a frozen cube of ice in her and the sensation of licking her pussy whilst freezing cold didn't feel quite right, but I was still turned on, particularly as she was sat on my face, which I love. It also showed that she was really open to trying new things.

One anniversary, she had dressed up for me, wearing an Octoberfest style dress that really showed off her cleavage. She gave me the most amazing blowjob and surprised me by giving me a kiss straight after with my cum still in her mouth. Even though I had already cum, she was quick enough that I was still really turned on. All I could say afterwards was 'that was fucking hot'.

We had talked a few times about going to a fetish club to see what it's like and hopefully have a bit of a play.

We found one locally and agreed to head down for a Halloween event. Cat was dressed as a sexy witch and me as a demon. We were really nervous heading down and felt a bit silly in fancy dress in the taxi, but we quickly settled in. The people there were really friendly and helped us to ease in.

We had a look around and got hot looking at the action happening in the dungeon area, but both of us were not feeling confident or dominant enough to take the other in for a play. I also think that aside from Cat enjoying a good hard spank or hair pulling during rough sex, that neither of us are really that into BDSM.

We were a little disappointed to find that the club rules were no nudity from the waist down and no sex, so we headed home after a few hours to have a marathon session well into the early hours.

We started to look further afield and found a fetish club in London that was not so strict on the activities. They also had a couples only area where you could get down to it without single guys wanking around you, (didn't realise this was a thing, but evidently so).

We booked into a gorgeous hotel nearby with a great big room that Cat still describes it as a very sexy hotel.

We got ready and headed down. This place was great with loads of stunning people dressed from quite tame right through to full latex suits and everything in between.

We watched some of the burlesque shows and later, whilst chilling in the bar area, saw an Asian girl push a guy onto the sofa in front of everyone, straddle him and start riding. Cat whispered in my ear 'that's so sexy'. Unfortunately, a guy started wanking right next to them which probably added to his stage fright. It finished as soon as it started.

We headed up to the couple's room, which was heaving with people licking, suckling and riding everywhere. It was very sexy, but also a little overwhelming. We found a spot and feeling a bit unsure if I could sustain an erection, I got down on my knees and started licking at her clit to get her off, with people sat either side of us. I loved being in this submissive position with people all around us.

We found a bit more space later on, this time she got

on her knees and took my now hard cock in her mouth. The couples only policy had seemed to ease off by this time and a guy motioned to me indicating he would like to join us. Whilst I would have loved him to, we had not discussed this and didn't want to scare Cat too soon.

I turned her round and bent her over the balcony railings, looking down over the club as I fucked her senseless.

We headed back to the hotel where we kept at it until the sun was up.

We tried another fetish club in London around 6 months later, but found it not as exciting and people not quite as friendly as the first, but we still had a bit of fun.

Things quieted down for some time after this. Cat became pregnant and gave birth to our wonderful son.

However, parenting was hard, especially when you're not getting any sleep for the first year.

Cat was still the same wonderful and sexy woman, but was self-conscious of the changes to her body following child birth. She was and always has been incredibly sexy to me.

It's fair to say I'd let myself go, piling on weight from regular takeaways in the first year of parenthood.

After the first year of parenting, we both decided to make an effort to eat better, drink less, stop smoking and exercise more.

Cat started becoming a lot more confident and our sex life certainly picked up.

I was still regularly fantasizing about her with another man, but struggling to tell her. One night, I was working away, got a bit drunk and spent the evening reading loving wife stories and watching cuckold porn and I was close to confessing my fantasy's by text. Thankfully, I resisted the urge.

We took a holiday and one night after a few drinks we started talking about sex. I finally plucked the courage to say it. That I wanted to bring someone else into our sex life, a man, and that I wanted to watch. Even though I'd had a few drinks, I was still very nervous of her response.

She listened and to my surprise started rubbing my leg, obviously getting turned on by my confession.

We finished our drinks and headed down to the empty beach in the middle of the night. We found a sun lounger and she rode me like a woman possessed. She eventually had to stop, as the arms of the sun laugher were rubbing her thighs, and 10 months later, she still has light scars from this.

We went back to the hotel and the rest of the holiday, I couldn't keep my hands off her. I'd confessed my deepest fantasy and she not only accepted it, was very turned on by it too!

Our sex life has been nonstop since then, I think

probably even more frequent than when we first got together.

I had talked more about my fantasies, that I would particularly see her with a black man and bought a huge realistic black dildo for her to play with. Its 9.5 inches long and 7 inches around.

It took Cat some warming up to take this dildo, but it is always worth the effort. I've heard her have some amazing orgasms over our time together, but the uncontrollable screaming when she orgasms from this cock is unlike anything I've seen before.

I was trying to figure out how to take things further. Cat wasn't keen on finding someone online, as was concerned about meeting some weirdo.

I was unsure about what the crowd might be like at swinger's clubs and thought Cat wouldn't be into getting it on with some middle aged guy. I also thought if I suggested it, she might think I was just trying to find an excuse to get with another woman.

Then one night, I was reading a story on here about a woman going to a black swinger's bar. I guessed it was just someone's fantasy, but I did a quick search online to find that there is a night in various venues across the UK called 'Black man's fan club'.

I read reviews and seems it was pretty well rated and had been running for some time. I found a venue about 45 minutes away and after a few drinks one night, suggested it to Cat.

Cat, I think was trying to keep me happy and agreed to go, but to my surprise suggested we go to the next event in 3 week's time. We fucked for hours that night, whilst talking about what might happen.

The next morning, before Cat woke up, I reserved our place online before either of us had a chance to get cold feet. It was set.

The next day at work, the realisation of this hit me and I could think of nothing else. My stomach was in knots with anxiety and excitement. It was going to be a long

3 weeks.

We had a few heart to hearts about our concerns and our limits. Cat said that she isn't into rimming, fair enough. She also reluctantly said that any sex should be protected, as we don't know the people. I agreed this was sensible and whilst I would love to see a big black guy fill her with cum, it's not worth the risk at this stage for someone we don't know.

I had said that the only limits I could think of is that if she wants to sleep with someone whilst I'm not there, ideally tell me first, ideally send me pictures, but certainly tell me afterwards, as otherwise it would feel like a betrayal.

We discussed our concerns about whether there would actually be black guys that would go, or whether I would want to see her with an old or overweight guy. I said that I want to see her with someone she was attracted to and if there wasn't anyone that fit the bill, we would just leave and go for a few drinks elsewhere.

The evening came round after what felt like forever. Cat got ready and looked absolutely stunning. She was wearing my favourite black satin corset that showed off her figure, along with jeans that would be replaced later with stockings and a short skirt. Her makeup looked sexy, she had really gone to town.

We drove there, both chatting about other things to distract us from the nervousness, until we got there. We sat in the car park for a few minutes and I was pleased to see a well-built black guy walk in as we were working up the courage.

We headed in and the staff were all very friendly. We were shown around to see a big social area with a bar and pool table. There was a small dark room with sofas and some porn playing on a screen. There was a huge open room with a giant bed in the middle and 3 small lockable private rooms.

We settled our nerves with a few drinks and a cigarette (we still have the occasional one). Looking around, there were a handful of black guys, and I was pleased to see most were around 30s and 40s. There were several couples, mostly 40s and 50s.

It was fair to say Cat was the hottest woman there and as such, a number of guys came and introduced themselves to us. One guy in particular, introduced himself as Mike. He was a little taller than me, maybe 6 feet, but had a really broad chest. He started chatting to us as we were in the locker room and made small talk. I think it was clear that we were first timers.

I thought he was attracted to Cat from our initial chat, but this was confirmed later when he came and sat next to us again. I was still feeling anxious about what might happen, but hoping something would. He wasn't being overly forward and was making nice conversation.

A bell rang, indicating it was time to dress down to underwear. We went back to the locker room to get prepared. I stripped down to my boxers and Cat asked me to help her with her suspenders. I felt really submissive bent down with others around, helping her to look sexy to hopefully have sex with another man.

We found a seat and started chatting when Mike came and sat on a sofa next to ours. I was sat in-between them, but he was clearly more interested in talking to Cat. I was thinking how to get them to sit next to each other, so decided to get us a drink and give them a moment.

When I came back, Mike was sat on my seat, but when he saw me returning, went to get up. I said not to worry and we kept on chatting. After our drinks, Cat suggested we take a look around to see what was happening.

We looked in the dark room and took a seat. Mike put his hand on Cat's leg. She put her hand on mine, looked at me and asked if I was ok with this. I smiled and said very happy and we kissed. She then turned and kissed Mike. There was definitely a twinge of jealousy at this point, but I was overwhelmed by the thought that this was actually going to happen.

Mike took Cat's hand under his towel and she started to stroke him. She reached into my boxers and stroked me too and Mike was working 2 fingers inside Cat.

Mike then suggested we go to a private room. We got in and the air was thick and humid. He stripped off and lay on the bed and told Cat to get him hard. She leaned over him and lowered her mouth to his cock.

Mike asked if I could see ok, obviously reading the situation well. I could make out in the mirror Cat sucking him, but it was dark so couldn't see clearly. I got behind cat and started fingering her now soaking wet pussy and kissed her ass. Mike was being quite aggressive, pulling her head down on his cock and I know she likes that. Mike then said, 'I really need to fuck you now'.

Cat bent over facing me and pulled at my boxers. I loved what was happening but despite popping a Viagra before we headed in, I was so overwhelmed that it was actually happening, I was struggling to get hard.

Mike got behind her and eased himself into her before building up pace and started pounding her hard. I really wanted to see him inside her, but loved seeing her face and how turned on she was. She was screaming hard and I was kissing her and telling her how sexy she was. Mike tried to get into her ass, but Cat stopped him, obviously a bit too big for her.

He then pulled her onto her side whilst spooning her from behind. He had a good pace and kept going for some time until he said he was going to cum. He pulled out and came on her ass.

He told her that she was amazing, that her ass was his kryptonite. He also said he needed to get a hotel room with her sometime to take her all night.

Mike got up, saying he needed to shower. I gave Cat a big kiss, telling her that was the sexiest thing I had ever seen. I really wanted to lick her ass clean, but couldn't bring myself to at that moment, my stomach still in knots.

We went to have another cigarette, I kept smiling at her. I needed the loo, so asked Cat if she could get us a drink.

When I came out, I couldn't find her at the bar. I was a little panicked looking around for her. someone at the bar said there were a lot of black guys that had gone off to one of the side rooms. I looked in the dark room, but no one there.

I looked in the private rooms, but all were empty. I went back to the bar and ordered a drink to settle my nerves. I then guessed she must be in the big open room. There was a lot going on in the big bed. I saw who I thought was Cat sucking a guy's cock. I waited by the side of the room, until I realised it wasn't her.

I went back to the bar to thankfully find her sat talking with Mike. She was very sorry for disappearing. Mike had dragged her off to the glory hole room (I'd forgotten about that one), and she had gathered a bit of an audience. She told me that she sucked him through the wall, before he came round and looked her cubicle. He fucked her from behind while other guys went into the other side, put their hands through the wall and started feeling her breasts.

As she was telling me this, I was rubbing her dripping

pussy whilst sat at the bar.

We went back to the sofas with Cat sat between me and Mike. We were chatting again, Mike made a few subtle innuendos and Cat called him on it. She was very flirty and guessed we would go back for another round soon.

Another black guy came and sat with us, I don't remember his name. He was polite enough, but Cat didn't seem to be drawn to him. He sat, trying to get in on the conversation several times, but not really reading the situation.

He suggested we all go and play tether on the big bed, but I started to get cold feet thinking it may be too much too fast. I told Mike that Cat and I needed a moment. We went to smoke again and agreed to call it a night. I got Mike's email and said I'd be in touch.

When we got home, my balls were aching. I hadn't been able to sustain an erection at the club, but was so turned on by what I'd seen. Cat rode me and I filled her with the biggest load of cum in my life.

I was still turned on and was rubbing her soaking pussy. I got between her legs and licked her cum filled pussy. I rolled her over and licked her ass where Mike had cum. There was none left but it still turned me on think he'd cum where my tongue was only a few hours ago.

We carried on fucking all weekend, recounting what had happened. Every time I thought about her and him together, I got a knot in my stomach that was only satisfied by cuddling up to her, kissing her, or sliding my cock inside her.

I emailed Mike to say thanks and that we'd both enjoyed his company and I'd enjoyed watching. I said maybe we'd meet up again.

Back at work on Monday, I could think of nothing else. I kept getting that knot in my stomach, but Cat wasn't there to ease it off. We spoke that night and she eased my mind, saying we didn't need to do anything more if either of us didn't want to.

By Wednesday, I was over it. I emailed Mike suggesting we get a hotel for the night. We now have a room booked for a couple of month's time and looking forward to our next adventure...

The Special Weekend Extravaganza

Justin had arranged thoroughly for their special weekend extravaganza, a fantasy that he had consistently nurtured somewhere inside his heart after taking his wedding vows. This was a wickedly lustful craving and a desperate want which he tried to fulfill in any case. With Emma by his side, he had successfully planned their kinky adventure this time; Justin felt as if he was flying the excitements of the indescribable paradise of fervor. In any case, Emma would have her own terms and twists to be explored during the kink session. That was what he profoundly adored and respected about her; her mysterious character, her hidden strategies and unpredictable methods that constantly flamed the passion in him. In this way, just the day after their grand wedding reception, they took a much-needed vacation. They arrived at Emma's uncle's estate in Bordeaux, France. The household servants were already sent on holiday leave for the weekend, the two lovebirds were all set and excited to encounter the ecstatic heights of their sensual fantasies. That was one hell of a night that turned Justin's marriage upside down.

Emma had a splendid spark of magnificent beauty,

enticement and elegance. Her thick, long, dense and blonde hair streamed behind her like the consistent waves of a cascade. Her skin was lustrous, brilliant and shone like molten gold, abundant like rich milk and cream. She had a statuesque shape in her tall, curvaceous and seductive body with bosoms the size of melons. Her butt was just like the splendidly hemispherical scoops of ice-creams. Justin at whatever point would see them in her tight, shape fitting skirt, would consistently drool to devour them that way and even spurt condiments all over that succulent booty to eat off for throughout the day. The scene occurred during one of the evenings when Emma overwhelmed Justin, dominated him and fulfilled his dreams.

Emma commanded Justin to position himself on the edge of the bed with his legs dangling. The enticing grin with a touch of insidiousness was sufficient for Justin to acknowledge. At that point, she restrained both of his legs spreading them wide separated like a "V" and tied them high up on the post of the bed. While his butts laid on the edge of the bed, his knees and ankles were broadly spread and bound with leather straps onto the bedposts making the "V" shape. In a similar manner, his hands also were extended wide apart and Emma tied his wrists onto the other two bedposts. At the point when she completed her aesthetic work of subjugation,

Emma laughed wickedly: "God, I can't recognize my very own talents. Brilliant, wouldn't you concur, my love?"

Under those conditions, Justin was so overpowered fantasizing the forthcoming kink plays that he could just swallow hard and nodded his affirmation. Emma prodded, "Would you like to know from where I crafted this excellent bondage, my love?" Justin's lips trembled and he whimpered: "Yes!" She proceeded: "From a BDSM site. I simply improvised the restraints as I blended them with my own ideas. God! I can't believe this position would grant such extraordinary access to your rear. Are you able to move, my love?" When Justin attempted to pull on the leather bondage by lifting his butt off the bed, the restrictions grasped him legs further firmly. Emma laughed at his silly endeavors. At the point when Justin curved his back and flexed his arms to lift his chest and upper body, the cuffs restrained his wrists more tightly. As goosebumps coursed through his restrained servile body, he was unable to accept how vulnerable he was with his lady love. "No...I can't!" Justin's lips trembled. Emma rushed to react, "That is so extraordinary. After all, we certainly wouldn't want our kinky adventure to end too soon and prematurely, do we? Now, since you agreed to play according to my wishes and desires, so from now on to the end of your life, you're my slave. Obviously, I have enslaved you, entranced you before...But from now on your role in our relationship is sealed." 'Slave', yes; Justin was the slave of his own savage wants and twisted perversions. He murmured with trembling lips: "Truly, my Queen!"

As she strolled around to the side of the bed, Justin lifted his head to watch his deviously enchanting tormentor. She looked incredible and thrilling wearing black silk, laced merry widow and G-string with matching stockings and heels. Casually resting adjacent to him, Emma lifted her right leg and settled her foot next to his head while her luscious lips wrapped up around the glass of her favorite potent and solid luxurious smell of her silky dress, he felt profoundly intoxicated. He looked at the mind-blowing sight of her long attractive legs exotically clad in black leggings. At that point, setting a hand underneath his head, Emma helped him to lift his head. As she brought the wine glass to his lips, she expressed, "Here, taste it. It's incredible!" But before he could taste the exquisitely flavorful beverage, his lips tasted the sweetness of her lipstick on the rim of the glass. Justin was shuddering to anticipate the upcoming sensational and wildly passionate encounters. After he sipped the red wine, he was somewhat relaxed and Emma winked. The glass was half full when she drew it away from his lips and kept it on the bedside table. At that point, she swung her legs and straddled him. Inclining forward, she eagerly peered into his eyes. Justin was somewhat mesmerized and got enraptured in her lustful eyes. His lady, the gem of woman with whom he pledged to spend the rest of his life and with whom he had spent endless pleasurable evenings, with whom he shared every mystery, whom he revered like a living goddess, and whom he always believed to know like the lines of his palm was still so mysterious and secretive to him. Things had just begun unfolding and Justin was already leaking his excitements from his half-erect organ. Emma inclined forward and kissed him profoundly. As his lips touched hers, he could sense the fire in her soul. As their tongues entangled, that fire vanquished his perverted and wild temptations. As a result, within moments, he just forgot whose air he was breathing in.

Inclining further, Emma carried her succulent bosom to his face. Her passionate desires and expectations were unmistakably demonstrated by her activities. Gradually, Justin lifted his head and began to caress, kiss, and nudge the valley in the middle of her voluptuous chest mounds. "Good boy!" Emma mumbled. As she reclined back just a little out of the range of his yearning lips, Justin battled against his bondage. She laughed again and asked, "Would you like to kiss them, slave?"

"Indeed, my Queen". He answered and swallowed.

"Great, if you can impress me with your job, I'll surely reward you," Emma teased. Then she inclined forward again and brought her sufficient chest mounds inside the region of his servile mouth, however keeping up the strains on his bondage. As Justin kissed and sucked on her right bosom, he detected the nipple hardening through the lacey cup of the corset. He detected that she shuddered with enthusiastic fervors and groaned softly. Within the next few moments, his tongue was circling the borders of her areola all the while sucking and kissing the nipple. Justin proceeded with his devoted sensual tributes pleasuring her tits. Gradually, his shoulders began to surrender to the restrictions imposed on him and he was losing the strength of his dedicated oral services. Detecting that like an accomplished dominatrix, Emma placed two cushions underneath his head encouraging him. Encouraged by her enormous help, Justin expanded his suction on her nipples. He opened his mouth to take in a greater amount of her covered tits. He sucked hard on every one of her delicious chest mounds like a hungry baby, filling his mouth and utilizing his tongue over her areola. The warmth from their skin-to-skin touch was consuming her as Justin detected the moisture in between her legs. Accordingly, his shaft twitched and he envisioned what he would and could have done if his hands were allowed to react to the invitation of her body. Hardly was he able to understand the amount of time he devotedly spent loving her succulent udders. Justin then kissed, slurped, and licked on her bosom until Emma had reclined. At that point, she settled his head in the cleavage of her voluptuous udders and squeezed her bosoms together. Justin smelled the inebriating fragrance of her cleavage entrancing his senses and to some degree chocking him. At that point, she again guided his head onto her nipples and through the silk texture; Justin exquisitely worshipped her abundant bosoms. They were all stained immediately showing his devoted oral ministrations. Reluctantly, Emma liberated herself from his mouth while still laying on him.

Emma laughed: "Excellent job, my slave. You did excellent and have earned a reward. Now, untie the straps on this corset, use your tongue. If you can do it, I'll remove it. Deal?" Likewise, Emma again inclined forward and Justin continued his devoted oral services. This merry laced widow was structured with front laces and the laces were settled in the middle of her bosoms. "You are so natural, slave!" His tormentor murmured into his ear. Justin groaned softly while he looked into his reflection in her eyes. And, with a delighted shush, Emma, planted a delicate kiss on his shoulders, sending another wave of shuddering goosebumps through the swampy profundities of his perverted and lust infected psyche. Emma then guided his head onto her laced corset and Justin began working his teeth onto the knots. But as usual, she was mysteriously adventurous; she stretched forward, laying her weight on him and drew her legs near the vicinity of his leaking erection. Justin had quite recently begun his advancement with the knots of her corset when Emma wickedly played her devious ploy absolutely baffling his senses. "Just continue working, my slave. Don't allow your Queen a chance to divert you", Emma teased. The more he unfastened the knots of her corset, the closer she drew her legs towards his leaking erection. It was clear she was purposefully prodding him. After he had unknotted the last knot, all Justin needed to do was to drag the lace and untie it totally. Yet, right at the moment, Emma drew her legs onto his pole and began to caress it with her foot. As he trembled to shake the whole bed, she smiled shrewdly distracting his ministrations. He was excessively desperate and in a rush to finish what he was ordered to do. But, sadly, that lace was too long to be in any way untied utilizing his teeth. Emma detected his bitter struggles and after ten tussling minutes, she positioned herself in a comfortable position for his slave. "Great job," acknowledged his Queen. "Now you can dispose of the laces, so you do it", she commanded. Utilizing his tongue and teeth, Justin got the end of the lace and dragged it through the eyelets. Obviously, with each passing eyelet, the ribbon grew longer and it was intensely difficult for Justin to proceed with his services. Yet, at last, he had pulled the lace totally from the corset nearly uncovering her succulent bosoms. The tedious procedure had totally depleted him and he was gasping fast in an incredible blend of fervor and weariness. Miserably attempting to uncover her bosoms and too drained to even think about working his tongue and teeth any further, Justin lay nibbling an end of her corset.

"Great! You never gave up. Now, let me dispose of this thing for you." Emma asserted.

At that point, Emma began to undress as she loosened the straps from the stockings and the corset. Finally, she totally uncovered the upper part of her tempting body. However, she was still in her panties. Justin was entranced at the captivating sight as he witnessed her pink nipples on her voluptuous chest mounds. Leaning forward, Emma placed one in his mouth. Emma then demanded, "That is your next chore slave. Worship my tits with your tongue, prove your love once again, show your longing to please me and make me cum. At that point, I might treat you with a reward." Over the months, as Justin had known Emma, she was a very sensuous lady. Most likely, one out of a thousand who savored amazing climaxes simply through breast stimulations only. Obviously, Justin needed to learn dedicatedly to work his tongue, lips, and teeth in that exquisite style that would please and delight her whenever they were intimate. Furthermore, when he graduated from her school of seduction, Justin had exhibited her mind-blowing climaxes on many occasions. Be that as it may, it took tremendous persistence, effort, and time to push Emma over the edges of excitement.

Within minutes, his mouth, lips, and tongue restarted their oral ministrations on her bosoms. Rhythmically, his mouth sucked and nibbled while his tongue flickered over her nipples energizing her exceedingly. Justin continued flickering his worn-out tongue on her nipples like a crazy baby. The stiffness of her nipples exhibited the fire in her spirit. At the point when he tugged at it with his teeth, Emma groaned in ecstasy and Justin detected her moistening further. Repeatedly and rhythmically, Justin kept flickering and sucked on both her nipples, while Emma shuddered down her spine detecting electric stimulations. Slowly and steadily, Justin felt her breath and pulse quickened. At the point when she shivered, Emma hollered out in passionate ecstasy. Justin pulled hard on one of her nipples while she encountered her first climaxes for the late evening sending her to the zeniths of her excitements. He was briefly depleted while she lay over him recuperating from the energetic fervors. Justin let her nipple gradually evade his mouth and relaxed up his head and exhausted mouth and tongue. While pasting fast, he breathed in her fascinating smell and the ecstatic delights she just encountered. At last, Emma raised herself, sat upon the bedside. She sipped her wine lazily. She also offered him a taste which he gulped briskly so as to quench his thirst. At the point when Justin saw her freshly saturated panties stained in overpowering lustful juices, his erection twitched, throbbed and leaked.

Emma acknowledged, "That was impressive, slave."

"Some folks don't give enough consideration to do foreplay and play with a lady's tits. They are simply in a rush to go to some different spots. I'm happy I trained you well. You have again earned your rewards. Your mouth needs some rest, right?" Emma prodded.

Justin answered, "Yes, my Queen".

Swinging her legs around, Emma straddled him facing his rear end. Her dazzling hemispherical scoop like ass cheeks was simply resting on his chest. Justin trembled in lustful excitements and savage wants when he detected and smelled her freshly moistened pussy lips through her underwear. Emma prodded, "Now, my slave, just relax and make the most of your reward." Reaching out to his horrendously anticipating erection with only two fingers, she stroked it. Gradually and relentlessly, Emma stroked his half-erect and leaking shaft. Her momentum appeared to him more like rolling her fingers over his throbbing erection as opposed to an enthusiastic and passionate handjob. Furthermore, as she moved her fingers over the veins of his organ, it sent electrifying stimulation all through his body hardening it to its full length and girth. His hips trembled as goosebumps coursed through his impatiently waiting body.

Justin heard her laughing and he groaned, "Fuck". Starting from the base, she moved her fingers gradually to the top measuring the length and girth of his solidified erection. At that point, Justin felt like Emma ran her long sexy fingers over the bulbous head of his pole and explored the fissure on its tip. At that point, again he felt like she stroked his hard and erect shaft descending back to the base. Like an accomplished dominatrix, she expertly proceeded with her tease while giving him some three-four snappy, quick and full strokes in between. Her ministrations were impeccable, balanced and proceeded in perfect rhythm. Justin was enticed to edge inevitably, yet his fervors were far away from release. Subsequently, Justin shuddered and groaned: "Oh God! Fuck! Fuck! Please, my Queen! Please let me cum!"

Emma utilized her fingers and cupped his balls and his

massaged pole which shook his body with electric stimulations. "I always wanted to tie and tease you till you're begging for a release", Emma affirmed. "I heard it makes men insane." She giggled. Those teasing minutes appeared to him like hours. Continually touching and invigorating him by her ministrations, yet never enough power to push him over the edge. At long last, her teases were excruciating and Justin frantically yearned to discharge his excitements.

"Please! Please, my Queen! I beg you! Please touch me harder, I have to cum," Justin pleaded.

"Try not to be reluctant to investigate your sexuality, fantasies, and wants. I realize how much you love them. I need to make them our own. They will bind us together. Don't be afraid, don't feel insecure or negative about your absolute submission and my sheer dominance. Under my dominance, control, and savage desire, you'll want for me. I'll show how I'll command you instead of murmuring in your ears. And as the play proceeds, your sole existence will be consumed by my seduction; your musings will be vanquished by the perverted desire to pleasure my curves and pits. Also, you'll fall further and more profound into your submission. I'll make you evolve. You'll abandon your old self, and become mine. To satisfy me will become your pleasure, your priority, and your sole meaning of life." Emma prodded in a way entrancing Justin.

"Please," Justin pleaded once more.

"Shhh!" she shushed, "Just relax and make the most of your reward. After all, you've earned it."

"Please, if you please! My Queen," Justin begged once more.

"OK, we should play a game. You stay silent while I give you a handjob. On the off chance that you do, you'll have what you desperately seek for the moment. However, if you utter a single word, well..." Justin heard Emma chuckling deviously and afterward, she continued her torturous slow and steady stroking. In spite of the fact that he complied with her in a split second, his body was trembling as goosebumps raced through his skin. It was practically impossible for Justin to withstand her teases and suppress his passionate excitements. Undoubtedly, her pace and power never enabled him to have what he desperately craved for that minute. By the by, her passionate torments were turning him on. Justin began to gasp breathing quicker and with each stroke, he was increasingly on edge and anxious to encounter his release. When her cautious and careful ministrations brought him right to the edge of an exceptional climax, Justin couldn't help himself and groan softly, "Oh! Fuck, yes my Queen! Yes, please..."

Promptly, Emma wrapped the fingers of both her hands over his pole and balls and gave him one final full stroke with full contact. Justin shivered and anticipated to encounter his first intense release of the night. Be that as it may, her holds on his ball and shaft increased to the point of excruciating torment restricting his release. Then, Emma un-mounted him and ceased her teasing ministrations.

"I win, slave!" Emma proclaimed. A little drop of pre-cum got away through his pole. Biting her lips, Emma gathered the protein juice drop onto the tip of her forefinger and carried it to his lips. Her indications were loud and clear. In this manner, without any protest, Justin simply licked the sparkling drop from at the tip of her finger.

"I hope your mouth have been sufficiently rested, my slave?" Emma inquired.

"Yes, my Queen," Justin replied terribly frustrated at the denial of his own climax.

"Great, then let's get it back to work. So, since I have won, you'll utilize your mouth and tongue to get me off once more," Emma commanded, "However, you'll do it over my panties".

"I need to taste you," Justin begged.

"Oh! My dear slave! You'll, but only if you do what I command." Emma concluded.

Justin saw the enthralling sight of her pussy lining from her freshly drenched panties. Probably, he had drooled for a moment of sheer distress to utilize his tongue exploring every last inch of her honey pot. And, when Justin breathed in her musky smell, it set off extreme raw passion. Usually, Emma liked to keep herself clean from pubic hairs (besides, Justin loved it that way) and when Emma straddled his face, he understood she had devised her enticing plots a long time before she even let him know. Without saying any further word, Justin worked his lips within her thighs. Then, he was going insane in raw desire and enraptured by the inebriating smell of her juices; he worked his way to the ridge where her thighs joined her body. As Justin kissed and licked up the edge, he detected Emma shuddering ecstatic delights flooding through her veins.

Obviously, as a woman of lush seduction, Emma consistently savored the incitements brought about by her slave's tongue, directly in her blessed hole. He smelled her, licked her through her panties, tasted her while his erection continued throbbing and twitching continually. Justin was going insane; his tongue was so near meet her magnificent Holy Grail, yet so far; only a slender silk fabric walling his tongue's worthy reunion. Overwhelmed by sheer distress, he carried his mouth to lower down offering his oral tributes on her covered pussy. Justin kissed and licked her exploring his tongue between her pussy and her anal pit. At last, in sheer enticement, he flawlessly worked his tongue separating her drenched panties from her pubic mounds. He detected the enthusiasm in her body, the savage lust in her mind and the fire in her spirit when he tasted the warmth and moisture in her pussy. Be that as it may, when he guided his tongue to make a deep plunge her lust, Emma stopped him.

Emma stated sternly, "No, not all that soon, my slave. I'm the one in control here. I'll reward you with my command to kiss my naked pussy. But, I'm certain you're dying to suck it, kiss it and fuck it with your tongue, right?

His voice sounded fuzzy when Justin answered, "Yes, my Queen. I want it more than anything at this moment."

"More than your own climax?" she teased back.

His pole jerked at her seductive probing. As it hadn't discharged its excitements, it was hard. And, for a minute, Justin thought inwardly, that Emma was riding him without letting him penetrate her. She was seducing him with her mere words, continually keeping him on the edge, yet never permitting his most prized reward. As Justin was too consumed by his very own steamy fascinations, he could just nod.

Emma reacted, "Be careful what you wish for. You don't have the foggiest idea when you get it. Now, eat my pussy. And, take as much time as is needed as I'm not going anywhere else, not tonight."

At that point, Justin followed her commands and proceeded with his lovely work. He tongued her delectable pussy mounds from top to bottom. Actually, his tongue nibbled the sensitive inside of her thighs in the middle of his lustful investigations and alluring oral ministrations. At the point when a soft groan got away from her throat, he detected that Emma also was getting turned on by her sheer dominance and his supreme submission. Slowly and steadily, Emma crawled nearer and carried her pussy and clit to his mouth. All Justin could breathe in was the stirring fragrance of her rosebuds; all his lips and tongue investigated, kissed and sucked were her shrouded rosebuds. Stroking his tongue up the silken fabric covering her pussy mounds, his tongue investigated her clit through the fabric. Justin took the time to suck her clits through the silk fabric. His tongue got more skilled as Emma rode him like her pet.

Emma attested, "Get in there and inhale deep. You won't get fresh air for some time. Do you love being my butt-sniffing toy, a pussy munching pet?"

Justin reacted by slurping on her rosebuds. As his tongue encircled and slurped her pussy mound, he detected her pussy pulsating. Emma grabbed his head, nearly immobilizing it. And afterward, inside minutes, Justin felt her orgasming to his tongue tributes. While his lips continued caressing her rosebuds, his tongue danced to and fro. Subsequently, Emma shivered in one more thrilling climax. Under extreme fervors, Emma unyieldingly squeezed her pussy into his mouth. She was groaning as if she was being exorcised. Realizing her electrifying stimulations, Justin stretched his mouth and took in her pussy, mons, and clits as much as he could. And, appropriately, he swayed his tongue sucking and licking her from base to top. When Emma had encountered one more sensational eruption, she released his head and reclined and lay on his shuddering body; Emma was already spent.

While she spent the following couple of moments gathering her strength and recuperating her from the three quick and successive sensual excitements, Justin was all the while slobbering to devour her totally. Indeed, he would never deny his obsession with his Queen and Goddess. At the point when she had recuperated, she got up and kissed him hard and profound. When their tongues got entrapped, they tasted each other's passionate and wild lust. In the end,

Emma broke the kiss and exclaimed: "Wow! I'm impressed!"

Justin grinned back in affirmation.

Emma probed once more: "I believe I should remove my panties. No?"

Justin nodded accordingly and she snaked her fingers on the string of her underwear. However, she would not take it off. "How desperate are you to see my naked pussy?" Emma teased.

"I would do anything you ask, whatever you ask, please" Justin replied.

"Would you like a close-up shot?" Emma teased further.

"Oh! Indeed, my Queen." Justin answered while his senses were absolutely hypnotized by her enticing tone, and anticipating his prized reward.

"And, you need to smell it, taste it. Don't you?" Emma asked teasingly.

"Yes, PLEASE," he breathed out in desperation.

What Emma expressed straightaway, totally baffled him.

"Alright, then how about we make a weekend deal. You

pleasure me with Cunnilingus before I take my morning shower, and this would be a daily schedule. You keep my fragrance all over your face and can't wash it before the day closes. The awesome aromatic smell of my pussy will transform you into a superior male; your increasingly perverted personality would link my juices and smell to my pleasure. Throughout the day you would consider pleasuring me. This is the thing that you truly crave for." Emma concluded.

Like always, Emma was as still unexplored and so undiscovered. What's more, when she directed her terms, his leaking erection throbbed and provoked consuming all his senses, he could only nod his head. The deal was finalized. Before long once more, Emma straddled his chest. Her pussy was simply inches away from his face; a little teasing separation. Be that as it may, when Justin lifted his face to offer his oral tributes once more, he found his explorations were beyond his boundaries. Emma grinned wickedly at his desperation and heaped up another cushion back of his head. Yet at the same time, her Holy Grail was beyond his reach. That is when Justin sensed it was her ploy to keep him right on the edges of excitements. Emma simply wanted him to inhale the mesmerizing fragrance of her sacred spot but then, never let him taste her naked pussy.

"Well," Emma murmured, "Too bad. So you'll have to

watch it since you can't reach it." Then she snaked her fingers and prodded her nipples. She cupped one of her bosoms and lifted it up to her mouth. Justin observed helplessly as she moved her tongue orbiting her nipple and areola. One of her hands proceeded with the teasing nipple play on her upper body. Her other hand, slowly and steadily, descended over her clit. In an impeccable rhythm, she pushed her middle finger in her pussy, kept thrusting in and out while her other hand and tongue continued with her nipple play. The appealing, sensual, and attractive exhibition of a seductive nipple play was irresistible to Justin and he ogled her provocative ministrations, spellbound.

He could just witness as she finger fucked herself and played with her succulent boobs. Emma continued toying with his mind while Justin continued drooling as a little pup sedated underneath her aroused lush framework. He was getting seriously frustrated and disappointed at the horniness developing in his veins and his pent-up sexual wants. Meanwhile, Emma shivered once more, her breathing got erratic and groaned in ecstasy. Once again, she had crossed the zenith of her sexual fervor and her middle finger came out sparkling in her juices. Her juices flooded his chest area, yet never arrived at his mouth.

"Please, my Queen... May I taste it," Justin begged.

"So you like to taste my juices, once more?" Emma teased.

"Yes, please!" He replied.

"Do you smell my pussy?" Emma teased back.

"Yes, I can, however, I need to taste you once more," Justin was practically teary.

"Then you'll suck all the juices from my pussy. Okay?" She prodded.

"Oh! Yes, my Queen," Justin answered with trembling lips.

"Great, then taste your Queen," Emma replied.

As her shimmering fingers settled over his slobbering mouth and tipped downward, Justin involuntarily opened his mouth wide to get her scrumptious juices. When her juices trickled into his gaping mouth, he devoured them as if he was thirsty for ages.

"That is sufficient for the time being," she concluded.

"Please, more please!" Justin begged.

"Shhh! Try not to distract me, let me enjoy," she asserted.

"But, I'm so desperate to taste you, please..." he begged once more.

"Okay, you're desperate to taste me, and I want you to be quiet. I just have the right tool to solve this dilemma," Emma answered teasingly and seductively.

At that point, she got up, inclined aside and reached out to the cabinet of the bedside table. From that point Emma hauled out a pink ball-gag mounted on a pink leather strap. She exclaimed: "How cute, isn't it? I got this from LoveHoney.com, particularly for this erotic holiday adventure." Justin remained bewildered. He witnessed her wild desire, fascinated. From there on, Emma straddled him once again. Nearly mesmerized, Justin watched her as she seductively scoured the ball of the gag over her labia. He watched her nearly enraptured as she bit her lips and quickly inserted the ball into her splashing pussy. It turned out lustrous, shimmering and wet with her juices.

"You needed to taste your Queen. So, taste your Queen," Emma stated.

As he tasted her volcanic lust from the ball gag, Emma squeezed the gag into his mouth. When Justin shut his eyes for a minute devouring her taste, Emma secured the lash behind his head. Justin was so consumed in savoring her taste that he licked and sucked the gag gobbling every drop of her delectable juices.

"God, I'm so horny... I need a cock inside me now,"

Emma teased.

Once more, his eyes widened and his heart pounded faster with the expectation of a powerful sexual penetration. At that point, she got up and settled herself right beside him. Her serious look examined each wrinkle on his skin; her extraordinary gaze probed every mole on his skin. Furthermore, when Emma laughed at his desperation, goosebumps overwhelmed his skin shivering his whole body. She reached out for his leaking erection and gradually began to give him a handjob. Her movements were too slow to even feel as her hand and fingers moved just once or twice per minute. Once in a while, her fingertips would simply lay on his erection and make no further movements. And on other occasions, Emma would rest the tip of her thumb on the bulbous head of his pole and grasp the length with the rest of her fingers. And then once in a while, Emma would prod him by cupping the head of his erection in the palm of her hand and snaking the fingers of her other hand on his scrotum.

When Justin would get too tempted to release his excitements and shake his hips in frustration and desperation, Emma would prod: "Just relax, my slave."

Emma always loved to tease Justin, both in and out of the bedroom. She would secretly love to crawl into his mind, heighten his perverted enticements and help him to achieve the summit of excitement. Be that as it may, this Emma was somebody whom Justin hardly knew. With every passing minute, she was becoming intensely addictive with her provocative techniques and excitingly erotic ploys. Clearly, it was impossible for Justin to withstand her slow and arousing cock teases. Despite the fact that her ministrations went on for around fifteen to twenty minutes, those minutes appeared to him like fucking hours; always dragging him to the summit of excitement, yet never enabling him to tumble off the edges. At long last, Emma settled her left hand with all the fingers grasping his scrotum and pulling it hard while with the fingers of her other hand she continued measuring the full length of his pole.

As Emma moved upward the erection, she applied the very faintest pressure Justin could ever imagine to have existed on earth. He shut his eyes feeling lost in an ocean of orgasm denial, her balls were heavy, and they were excruciatingly painful, yet strongly turned on by her prodding ministrations. At that point, Emma ground the erection with full pressure descending downward and when she detected his pole throbbing and pulsating, she broke all contact. With enticing astonishment filling her eyes, Emma watched his pole releasing the drops of pre-cum while she bit her lips and laughed at her lovely and flawless cock teases.

Step by step, his situation was worsening and his breathing quickened; Justin felt his heart pounding like drums, yet, he was no place closer to encounter his animating ejaculations.

Examining further and feeling proud at her stunning work, Justin heard Emma chuckling wickedly, "Perfect, nice and hard. Much the same as I needed it to be. Now, how about we keep it that way?"

While his eyes were still shut, Justin detected her reaching at the bedside table cabinet once again and hauling out another toy. At the point when Justin opened his eyes, he was stunned to discover that she had a cock ring to tease him with. The ring was formed like the number "8" and was probably 1-inch wide. Emma expertly worked the ring with one side snapping his scrotum that pushed the balls to the end of his pole, while the opposite side snapped the base of his hardened erection. Justin inhaled faster experiencing the limits of his erection and muffled groans got away from his throat through the gag.

Now, Emma began her teases vigorously. His balls began to ache and the torment was horrifying, continually tempting and pleading for an ejaculation. Before long, Emma followed with long, slow strokes up and down his shaft. Once in a while, in between her ministrations, Emma would let her long, sexy fingers to scratch the delicate underside of his pole and the bulbous head. Once in a while, one of her hands would cup his scrotum while the other would stroke his erection; neither fast nor even sufficient pressure. And, most importantly, never let her slave reach the pinnacle of his excitement. Therefore, the agony in his balls developed unbearably and they swelled inside the restrictions of his scrotum. Emma's touches became unbearable as time passed and Justin moaned in his ball gag gasping faster and harder.

"Relax... slow down... Just relax. Give my voice a chance to stream over and within you for the next 30 minutes. There's nothing else that matters. It's just you and my voice. I'll take as much time as necessary. I'll lift you up, lead you and make you sit on the throne of sexual ecstasy. I'll run my hands down your spine. I'll grab you by the nape of your neck and kiss you for the last time. You'll forget whose air you're inhaling. Kiss you thoroughly. This is as close as two bodies can get, figuratively, and truly. It's not about making you groan or scream, it's about making you forget how to breathe. I'll make these minutes and seconds matter. I'll make you recall. It is not a race. I'll leave my mark on your body. I'll leave my mark on your heart and memory. I'll lead you to ride the delights of euphoria. More profound, more slow, longer. I'll make heat where our bodies will meet. There's energy. There's sex. There's adoration. And afterward, there is this... The smell of my hair, the flavor of my mouth, the feeling of my skin, appeared to have conquered every one of your senses and gotten inside you or into the air around you. I've become your absolute necessity." Emma stated as she burned in sheer lust and dominance.

Perhaps, Emma too detected his agony and before long changed what she was continuing for quite a long time. Lifting his cock with her hand, Emma took the bulbous cock head into her mouth. Justin shuddered when he felt her delicate, soft, and luscious lips and warm tongue wrapping his erection. Before long, Emma had begun a long and slow blowjob. Sucking hard, Emma wrapped her lips and tongue all around and welcomed a greater amount of his erection in her mouth. Her cheeks hollowed in suction and she slurped like a young girl on a candy. At that point, as her suction increased, she held him there in her mouth. Gradually, Emma slid up his erection in an excruciatingly slow movement. When she arrived at the head, Emma utilized her tongue slurping on the head of his pole and then she kept on invading his erection somewhere down in her throat. As Justin was approaching the pinnacle of his sensual excitements slowly and steadily, his breathing got erratic.

She probably detected his erection throbbing and pulsating while Justin moaned like a pig on his ball gag.

Accordingly, Emma ceased her oral ministrations and patiently waited for a few minutes to let his excitement calm down. Justin's world was almost deaf and dumb because all he could hear was his heart pounding like bass drums and impatiently waiting for Emma to resume her oral teases. Once again, she brought him right to the edge and suddenly stopped making him all the more frustrated. This continued for several agonizing minutes. Then she proceeded with her enchanting ministrations on his scrotum. Emma licked them and sucked them into her mouth greasing them up in her saliva while her fingers stroked his manhood. And again, when he was spot on the edge of his excitements, Emma ceased unexpectedly frustrating him beyond his imaginations while he frantically begged for a climax. This continued for almost five to six times before Emma got bored. Or perhaps, she a different devious thought just crossed her mind.

Emma stared at him and asked: "Would you like to fuck your Queen?"

Justin moaned in his mouth gag accordingly.

"Alright, blink your eyes twice, if it's a 'YES'", she commanded.

Justin blinked twice to acknowledge.

"I hope you remember the rules, isn't that so? I'm the

one in control here. In the event that you don't comply with your Queen, you don't have the faintest idea regarding your punishment. Now, you'll obey me, don't you?" Emma inquired.

Justin again blinked his eyes twice in a hurry to confirm.

"Great," she said. "Now, I will loosen the straps on your ankles at bed level. Be that as it may, I don't want any untoward movement, OK?" she inquired.

Justin's eyes blinked twice involuntarily and hastily.

Then Emma moved to his ankles and unfastened the restrains and loosened the bondage on his knees. It felt like paradise to be released from the bondage. His butts were numb from the prolonged restrainment. Despite the fact that Justin had the choice to move his hips and thighs, he could barely lift himself more than half an inch from the bed. Then Emma again went after the cabinet in the bedside table and pulled out another toy. Justin was not able see what it was as she shrouded it behind her or might be, he was so desperate to have his releases that his mind never attempted to explore it any further. Then Emma straddled his bottom, kneeling, and slowly and steadily facilitated the head of his hardened erection into her greased cunt.

"I'll make you forget your name while you're occupied

with groaning mine. I swear I won't stop until your legs are shaking. I swear I won't stop until you scream my name to the neighbors. My greatest turn on is turning you on. You don't need polite love. You hunger for the realization that you are always in the hands of a lady who is capable of being excited, and who you excited to find that lady to finds you truly marvelous, to whose furious power and dominance and intense sexual appetite keeps you always enticed on the edge. You always want to be at the feet of a dominatrix. There's an ache that you can't control in a spot you can't name and it typically calls for my name. You're intoxicated by my fragrance and the manner in which I taste. You're addicted to the manner in which you lose yourself underneath my touch, to the manner in which your skin longs for a greater amount of me on it. You're intoxicated by the manner in which it feels fulfilled after we're finished." Emma declared seductively.

She began to descend gradually onto his erection, very slowly. Emma did it until her clits squeezed against the cock ring. For a brief minute, Justin couldn't help suspecting that she was proceeding with her teases even when she was riding him. In spite of the fact that it felt heaven when her delicate vaginal muscles devoured his erection, the moderate descent was making him insane. Then gradually she climbed onto his erection until the tip was simply touching her internal lips. When Justin attempted to hump from underneath in sheer desperation of his pent-up sexual desires, Emma shushed and alarmed: "You do it again, I'll leave you with blue balls till the next weekend."

A drop of tear flowed from his left eye as Justin clenched his eyes to withstand her provocative prods. Justin detected her lips on his eyelids as Emma kissed him there and affirmed: "We are not making love, my slave. I'm making you mine, just mine, and mine only. I want you to feel that you have a place with me, just me." When he felt her delicate lips his shoulders and neck, Justin trembled to anticipate her next tease. Of course, Emma gradually slid onto his erection and remained there for some minute. Those three movements most likely had taken three agonizing minutes and it appeared Justin had forgotten to keep track of time. Gradually, he sensed her pelvic muscle contract while her soaked pussy stroked his erection. Rhythmically, Emma contracted and loosened up her pelvic muscles while relaxing onto his erection. He panted faster, his senses got dumb and numb and Justin moaned on the ball gag as he watched his reflection in her salacious eyes.

"There are three and sixty-five things you are yet to find out about your wife. I'll tell you one every day. You chose to flip the switch of our relationship. Thus, this is traditional love no more, I'm your hardcore Mistress driving you to the craziest level of insanity, where your mind, body, and soul will break to pieces well before I'm done. Our experiences would be cruel, however, you would long for my brand of cruelty. I want to discover each hidden fantasy that you yearn to satisfy, and I have a thousand different ways to make you scream my name. I'm your Queen, the only reason for your existence. Along these lines, from now on, I'm going to take you, possess you, claim you, whenever, where ever and however I want. Does that thrill you?"

Justin blinked twice again to express his consent.

Then Emma brought forth the toy that she hid behind her back, a vibrator. Turning it on, she contacted her clit and Justin realized the frequencies resonating against his erection. Her impeccable skills forced him to accept that Emma was an expert Dominatrix, a seasoned manipulator. Her self-control and fearlessness were unbelievably astonishing; this Emma was in her new seductive avatar, an entirely different person whom Justin hardly knew. Then she snaked the vibrator onto the base of his erection while still pressing her cunt over it. Emma ascended his erection while rubbing the vibrator on her clit. Then she settled the vibrator onto his throbbing scrotum and the impact was unbelievably stimulating, it was electric.

The frequencies of the vibrator throbbed, his swollen

and excruciatingly hurting balls dragging him to his edges. Justin moaned and exactly when he was going to accomplish the summit of his fervors, Emma ceased and push herself with total power, her cunt devouring his erection once again. His hips shivered and his thighs trembled because again he was denied his peak of ecstasy. Every one of her teases and denials were unreasonably wild for Justin, always keeping him right on the edge and never letting him release his fervors. Thus, he was becoming increasingly impatient and frustrated. Emma was utilizing him as her toy; his mind, his desires, his wants were simply so immaterial, and all she craved for was her own pleasures and stimulations. Teasing his mind, crawling into it and fucking the hell out of it and taking all he had, yet giving him none.

Emma again slipped onto his erection and now her movements had a regular in and out rhythm. Be that as it may, once in a while, her entrances would be followed by fast withdrawal. Slowly and steadily, her thrusts were getting deeper and faster creating a pattern. But, she would stop in between and relax just to prolong the electric stimulations. Without a doubt, Justin was encountering the most disappointing and frustrating fucking he'd ever experienced. Perhaps, Emma positioned him directly on the edges of his fervors for around 30 minutes. Be that as it may, those

30 minutes seemed like infinity.

"Are you ready to come, my slave?" Emma asked while gradually ascending from his excruciatingly hurting erection.

Justin blinked his eyes twice, thrice, perhaps multiple times, which demonstrated his urgency. She laughed and breathed out: "You've been so excellent this entire night. My ideal man-toy. So, I'm permitting you the delight, however, remember that I'm not done yet."

At last, Justin realized her thrusts were guided by the reason to make him cum. He witnessed as her breathing got more erratic and harder and faster. Justin was dazzled to watch Emma riding his pole like a rodeo cowgirl and he realized his pole building a strain to throw him off the peaks of excitements. Emma fingered her clits like a bitch in heat and her eyes were clenched to feel the electric sensations. Inside minutes, she groaned with delight and reached the pinnacle of her excitements. Flooding juices of wild lust greased up his erection and she thrust and slapped her butts hard onto his crotches in a thrill. In any case, this time Emma didn't stop and Justin was lucky that she proceeded with her movements until he had encountered his stimulations too. Long, deep and erratic strokes continued as her vaginal muscles devoured and choked his erection and exploded him to an awesome invigorating climax. Justin moaned like a pig on his muffle encountering what he wanted the most that evening. It was the best fuck Justin had ever encountered in months and his whole body shook with the reverberating throbbing of his erection.

Emma, at long last, collapsed onto his chest experiencing her sensational delights of the highest heavens while Justin lay sedated underneath her encountering his very own sexual freedom. He didn't know how long they stayed like that completely immobilized. When Emma gazed up, Justin could even sense the burning lust in her eyes. She removed his mouth gag and planted a profound kiss on his lips and their faces flushed with adoration and joy. Their tongues met and they tasted each other's enthusiasm.

Emma broke first yet kept Justin's still hard erection somewhere deep inside her pussy.

"Amazing! Wow!" Emma murmured.

"How could you get so strong and dominated me for so long?" Justin breathed.

Emma winked and answered: "We do all have our secrets, isn't that right? Besides, I just played along once I entered my Dom headspace."

Also, yes the night and the days that followed, Justin

found more of her privileged insights, her secrets which
constantly made him want her more and crave for her
more.